SO HAUNTED

(A Faith Bold Mystery —Book Fourteen)

BLAKE PIERCE

Blake Pierce

Blake Pierce is the USA Today bestselling author of the RILEY PAGE mystery series, which includes seventeen books. Blake Pierce is also the author of the MACKENZIE WHITE mystery series, comprising fourteen books; of the AVERY BLACK mystery series, comprising six books; of the KERI LOCKE mystery series, comprising five books; of the MAKING OF RILEY PAIGE mystery series, comprising six books; of the KATE WISE mystery series, comprising seven books; of the CHLOE FINE psychological suspense mystery, comprising six books; of the JESSIE HUNT psychological suspense thriller series, comprising thirty-eight books (and counting); of the AU PAIR psychological suspense thriller series, comprising three books; of the ZOE PRIME mystery series, comprising six books; of the ADELE SHARP mystery series, comprising sixteen books, of the EUROPEAN VOYAGE cozy mystery series, comprising six books; of the LAURA FROST FBI suspense thriller, comprising eleven books; of the ELLA DARK FBI suspense thriller, comprising twenty-one books (and counting); of the A YEAR IN EUROPE cozy mystery series, comprising nine books, of the AVA GOLD mystery series, comprising six books; of the RACHEL GIFT mystery series, comprising fifteen books (and counting); of the VALERIE LAW mystery series, comprising nine books; of the PAIGE KING mystery series, comprising eight books; of the MAY MOORE mystery series, comprising eleven books; of the CORA SHIELDS mystery series, comprising eight books; of the NICKY LYONS mystery series, comprising eight books, of the CAMI LARK mystery series, comprising ten books; of the AMBER YOUNG mystery series, comprising eight books; of the DAISY FORTUNE mystery series, comprising five books; of the FIONA RED mystery series, comprising thirteen books (and counting); of the FAITH BOLD mystery series, comprising seventeen books (and counting); of the JULIETTE HART mystery series, comprising five books; of the MORGAN CROSS mystery series, comprising thirteen books (and counting); of the FINN WRIGHT mystery series, comprising seven books (and counting); of the new SHEILA STONE suspense thriller series, comprising eight books (and counting); and of the new RACHEL BLACKWOOD suspense thriller series, comprising eight books (and counting).

An avid reader and lifelong fan of the mystery and thriller genres, Blake loves to hear from you, so please feel free to visit

BOOKS BY BLAKE PIERCE

RACHEL BLACKWOOD SUSPENSE THRILLER
NOT THIS WAY (Book #1)
NOT THIS TIME (Book #2)
NOT THIS CLOSE (Book #3)
NOT THIS ROAD (Book #4)
NOT THIS LATE (Book #5)
NOT THIS NIGHT (Book #6)
NOT THIS PLACE (Book #7)
NOT THIS SOON (Book #8)

SHEILA STONE SUSPENSE THRILLER
SILENT GIRL (Book #1)
SILENT TRAIL (Book #2)
SILENT NIGHT (Book #3)
SILENT HOUSE (Book #4)
SILENT SCREAM (Book #5)
SILENT PREY (Book #6)
SILENT RITUAL (Book #7)
SILENT PRAYER (Book #8)

FINN WRIGHT MYSTERY SERIES
WHEN YOU'RE MINE (Book #1)
WHEN YOU'RE SAFE (Book #2)
WHEN YOU'RE CLOSE (Book #3)
WHEN YOU'RE SLEEPING (Book #4)
WHEN YOU'RE SANE (Book #5)
WHEN YOU'RE SILENT (Book #6)
WHEN YOU'RE GONE (Book #7)

MORGAN CROSS MYSTERY SERIES
FOR YOU (Book #1)
FOR RAGE (Book #2)
FOR LUST (Book #3)
FOR WRATH (Book #4)
FOREVER (Book #5)
FOR US (Book #6)

www.blakepierceauthor.com to learn more and stay in touch.

ISBN: 978-1-0943-8531-0

FOR NOW (Book #7)
FOR ONCE (Book #8)
FOR ETERNITY (Book #9)
FORLORN (Book #10)
FOR SILENCE (Book #11)
FORBIDDEN (Book #12)
FOR FEAR (Book #13)
FORSAKEN (Book #14)

JULIETTE HART MYSTERY SERIES
NOTHING TO FEAR (Book #1)
NOTHING THERE (Book #2)
NOTHING WATCHING (Book #3)
NOTHING HIDING (Book #4)
NOTHING LEFT (Book #5)

FAITH BOLD MYSTERY SERIES
SO LONG (Book #1)
SO COLD (Book #2)
SO SCARED (Book #3)
SO NORMAL (Book #4)
SO FAR GONE (Book #5)
SO LOST (Book #6)
SO ALONE (Book #7)
SO FORGOTTEN (Book #8)
SO INSANE (Book #9)
SO SMITTEN (Book #10)
SO SIMPLE (Book #11)
SO BROKEN (Book #12)
SO CRUEL (Book #13)
SO HAUNTED (Book #14)
SO SILENT (Book #15)
SO BLEAK (Book #16)
SO HOLLOW (Book #17)

FIONA RED MYSTERY SERIES
LET HER GO (Book #1)
LET HER BE (Book #2)
LET HER HOPE (Book #3)
LET HER WISH (Book #4)
LET HER LIVE (Book #5)

LET HER RUN (Book #6)
LET HER HIDE (Book #7)
LET HER BELIEVE (Book #8)
LET HER FORGET (Book #9)
LET HER TRY (Book #10)
LET HER PLAY (Book #11)
LET HER VANISH (Book #12)
LET HER FADE (Book #13)

DAISY FORTUNE MYSTERY SERIES
NEED YOU (Book #1)
CLAIM YOU (Book #2)
CRAVE YOU (Book #3)
CHOOSE YOU (Book #4)
CHASE YOU (Book #5)

AMBER YOUNG MYSTERY SERIES
ABSENT PITY (Book #1)
ABSENT REMORSE (Book #2)
ABSENT FEELING (Book #3)
ABSENT MERCY (Book #4)
ABSENT REASON (Book #5)
ABSENT SANITY (Book #6)
ABSENT LIFE (Book #7)
ABSENT HUMANITY (Book #8)

CAMI LARK MYSTERY SERIES
JUST ME (Book #1)
JUST OUTSIDE (Book #2)
JUST RIGHT (Book #3)
JUST FORGET (Book #4)
JUST ONCE (Book #5)
JUST HIDE (Book #6)
JUST NOW (Book #7)
JUST HOPE (Book #8)
JUST LEAVE (Book #9)
JUST TONIGHT (Book #10)

NICKY LYONS MYSTERY SERIES
ALL MINE (Book #1)
ALL HIS (Book #2)

ALL HE SEES (Book #3)
ALL ALONE (Book #4)
ALL FOR ONE (Book #5)
ALL HE TAKES (Book #6)
ALL FOR ME (Book #7)
ALL IN (Book #8)

CORA SHIELDS MYSTERY SERIES
UNDONE (Book #1)
UNWANTED (Book #2)
UNHINGED (Book #3)
UNSAID (Book #4)
UNGLUED (Book #5)
UNSTABLE (Book #6)
UNKNOWN (Book #7)
UNAWARE (Book #8)

MAY MOORE SUSPENSE THRILLER
NEVER RUN (Book #1)
NEVER TELL (Book #2)
NEVER LIVE (Book #3)
NEVER HIDE (Book #4)
NEVER FORGIVE (Book #5)
NEVER AGAIN (Book #6)
NEVER LOOK BACK (Book #7)
NEVER FORGET (Book #8)
NEVER LET GO (Book #9)
NEVER PRETEND (Book #10)
NEVER HESITATE (Book #11)

PAIGE KING MYSTERY SERIES
THE GIRL HE PINED (Book #1)
THE GIRL HE CHOSE (Book #2)
THE GIRL HE TOOK (Book #3)
THE GIRL HE WISHED (Book #4)
THE GIRL HE CROWNED (Book #5)
THE GIRL HE WATCHED (Book #6)
THE GIRL HE WANTED (Book #7)
THE GIRL HE CLAIMED (Book #8)

VALERIE LAW MYSTERY SERIES

NO MERCY (Book #1)
NO PITY (Book #2)
NO FEAR (Book #3)
NO SLEEP (Book #4)
NO QUARTER (Book #5)
NO CHANCE (Book #6)
NO REFUGE (Book #7)
NO GRACE (Book #8)
NO ESCAPE (Book #9)

RACHEL GIFT MYSTERY SERIES
HER LAST WISH (Book #1)
HER LAST CHANCE (Book #2)
HER LAST HOPE (Book #3)
HER LAST FEAR (Book #4)
HER LAST CHOICE (Book #5)
HER LAST BREATH (Book #6)
HER LAST MISTAKE (Book #7)
HER LAST DESIRE (Book #8)
HER LAST REGRET (Book #9)
HER LAST HOUR (Book #10)
HER LAST SHOT (Book #11)
HER LAST PRAYER (Book #12)
HER LAST LIE (Book #13)
HER LAST WHISPER (Book #14)
HER LAST SECRET (Book #15)

AVA GOLD MYSTERY SERIES
CITY OF PREY (Book #1)
CITY OF FEAR (Book #2)
CITY OF BONES (Book #3)
CITY OF GHOSTS (Book #4)
CITY OF DEATH (Book #5)
CITY OF VICE (Book #6)

A YEAR IN EUROPE
A MURDER IN PARIS (Book #1)
DEATH IN FLORENCE (Book #2)
VENGEANCE IN VIENNA (Book #3)
A FATALITY IN SPAIN (Book #4)

ELLA DARK FBI SUSPENSE THRILLER
GIRL, ALONE (Book #1)
GIRL, TAKEN (Book #2)
GIRL, HUNTED (Book #3)
GIRL, SILENCED (Book #4)
GIRL, VANISHED (Book 5)
GIRL ERASED (Book #6)
GIRL, FORSAKEN (Book #7)
GIRL, TRAPPED (Book #8)
GIRL, EXPENDABLE (Book #9)
GIRL, ESCAPED (Book #10)
GIRL, HIS (Book #11)
GIRL, LURED (Book #12)
GIRL, MISSING (Book #13)
GIRL, UNKNOWN (Book #14)
GIRL, DECEIVED (Book #15)
GIRL, FORLORN (Book #16)
GIRL, REMADE (Book #17)
GIRL, BETRAYED (Book #18)
GIRL, BOUND (Book #19)
GIRL, REFORMED (Book #20)
GIRL, REBORN (Book #21)

LAURA FROST FBI SUSPENSE THRILLER
ALREADY GONE (Book #1)
ALREADY SEEN (Book #2)
ALREADY TRAPPED (Book #3)
ALREADY MISSING (Book #4)
ALREADY DEAD (Book #5)
ALREADY TAKEN (Book #6)
ALREADY CHOSEN (Book #7)
ALREADY LOST (Book #8)
ALREADY HIS (Book #9)
ALREADY LURED (Book #10)
ALREADY COLD (Book #11)

EUROPEAN VOYAGE COZY MYSTERY SERIES
MURDER (AND BAKLAVA) (Book #1)
DEATH (AND APPLE STRUDEL) (Book #2)
CRIME (AND LAGER) (Book #3)
MISFORTUNE (AND GOUDA) (Book #4)

CALAMITY (AND A DANISH) (Book #5)
MAYHEM (AND HERRING) (Book #6)

ADELE SHARP MYSTERY SERIES
LEFT TO DIE (Book #1)
LEFT TO RUN (Book #2)
LEFT TO HIDE (Book #3)
LEFT TO KILL (Book #4)
LEFT TO MURDER (Book #5)
LEFT TO ENVY (Book #6)
LEFT TO LAPSE (Book #7)
LEFT TO VANISH (Book #8)
LEFT TO HUNT (Book #9)
LEFT TO FEAR (Book #10)
LEFT TO PREY (Book #11)
LEFT TO LURE (Book #12)
LEFT TO CRAVE (Book #13)
LEFT TO LOATHE (Book #14)
LEFT TO HARM (Book #15)
LEFT TO RUIN (Book #16)

THE AU PAIR SERIES
ALMOST GONE (Book#1)
ALMOST LOST (Book #2)
ALMOST DEAD (Book #3)

ZOE PRIME MYSTERY SERIES
FACE OF DEATH (Book#1)
FACE OF MURDER (Book #2)
FACE OF FEAR (Book #3)
FACE OF MADNESS (Book #4)
FACE OF FURY (Book #5)
FACE OF DARKNESS (Book #6)

A JESSIE HUNT PSYCHOLOGICAL SUSPENSE SERIES
THE PERFECT WIFE (Book #1)
THE PERFECT BLOCK (Book #2)
THE PERFECT HOUSE (Book #3)
THE PERFECT SMILE (Book #4)
THE PERFECT LIE (Book #5)
THE PERFECT LOOK (Book #6)

THE PERFECT AFFAIR (Book #7)
THE PERFECT ALIBI (Book #8)
THE PERFECT NEIGHBOR (Book #9)
THE PERFECT DISGUISE (Book #10)
THE PERFECT SECRET (Book #11)
THE PERFECT FAÇADE (Book #12)
THE PERFECT IMPRESSION (Book #13)
THE PERFECT DECEIT (Book #14)
THE PERFECT MISTRESS (Book #15)
THE PERFECT IMAGE (Book #16)
THE PERFECT VEIL (Book #17)
THE PERFECT INDISCRETION (Book #18)
THE PERFECT RUMOR (Book #19)
THE PERFECT COUPLE (Book #20)
THE PERFECT MURDER (Book #21)
THE PERFECT HUSBAND (Book #22)
THE PERFECT SCANDAL (Book #23)
THE PERFECT MASK (Book #24)
THE PERFECT RUSE (Book #25)
THE PERFECT VENEER (Book #26)
THE PERFECT PEOPLE (Book #27)
THE PERFECT WITNESS (Book #28)
THE PERFECT APPEARANCE (Book #29)
THE PERFECT TRAP (Book #30)
THE PERFECT EXPRESSION (Book #31)
THE PERFECT ACCOMPLICE (Book #32)
THE PERFECT SHOW (Book #33)
THE PERFECT POISE (Book #34)
THE PERFECT CROWD (Book #35)
THE PERFECT CRIME (Book #36)
THE PERFECT PREY (Book #37)
THE PERFECT BETRAYAL (Book #38)

CHLOE FINE PSYCHOLOGICAL SUSPENSE SERIES
NEXT DOOR (Book #1)
A NEIGHBOR'S LIE (Book #2)
CUL DE SAC (Book #3)
SILENT NEIGHBOR (Book #4)
HOMECOMING (Book #5)
TINTED WINDOWS (Book #6)

KATE WISE MYSTERY SERIES
IF SHE KNEW (Book #1)
IF SHE SAW (Book #2)
IF SHE RAN (Book #3)
IF SHE HID (Book #4)
IF SHE FLED (Book #5)
IF SHE FEARED (Book #6)
IF SHE HEARD (Book #7)

THE MAKING OF RILEY PAIGE SERIES
WATCHING (Book #1)
WAITING (Book #2)
LURING (Book #3)
TAKING (Book #4)
STALKING (Book #5)
KILLING (Book #6)

RILEY PAIGE MYSTERY SERIES
ONCE GONE (Book #1)
ONCE TAKEN (Book #2)
ONCE CRAVED (Book #3)
ONCE LURED (Book #4)
ONCE HUNTED (Book #5)
ONCE PINED (Book #6)
ONCE FORSAKEN (Book #7)
ONCE COLD (Book #8)
ONCE STALKED (Book #9)
ONCE LOST (Book #10)
ONCE BURIED (Book #11)
ONCE BOUND (Book #12)
ONCE TRAPPED (Book #13)
ONCE DORMANT (Book #14)
ONCE SHUNNED (Book #15)
ONCE MISSED (Book #16)
ONCE CHOSEN (Book #17)

MACKENZIE WHITE MYSTERY SERIES
BEFORE HE KILLS (Book #1)
BEFORE HE SEES (Book #2)
BEFORE HE COVETS (Book #3)
BEFORE HE TAKES (Book #4)

BEFORE HE NEEDS (Book #5)
BEFORE HE FEELS (Book #6)
BEFORE HE SINS (Book #7)
BEFORE HE HUNTS (Book #8)
BEFORE HE PREYS (Book #9)
BEFORE HE LONGS (Book #10)
BEFORE HE LAPSES (Book #11)
BEFORE HE ENVIES (Book #12)
BEFORE HE STALKS (Book #13)
BEFORE HE HARMS (Book #14)

AVERY BLACK MYSTERY SERIES
CAUSE TO KILL (Book #1)
CAUSE TO RUN (Book #2)
CAUSE TO HIDE (Book #3)
CAUSE TO FEAR (Book #4)
CAUSE TO SAVE (Book #5)
CAUSE TO DREAD (Book #6)

KERI LOCKE MYSTERY SERIES
A TRACE OF DEATH (Book #1)
A TRACE OF MURDER (Book #2)
A TRACE OF VICE (Book #3)
A TRACE OF CRIME (Book #4)
A TRACE OF HOPE (Book #5)

PROLOGUE

Art was all about contrast.

Melissa was probably the only sculptor she knew who understood that. Plenty of painters understood it. Photographers had come around to realizing that light wasn't the only aspect of an image. Architects had the basics down even if they weren't entirely aware why their minimalist, functional designs were so appealing.

But sculptors were all about fluidity. They insisted that everything needed to flow like water in order for a piece to be successful. Melissa didn't blame them. There was a certain satisfaction in making something hard and unyielding like marble seem soft and fluid like water. It demonstrated the artist's mastery over his craft.

It was also boring as hell.

Come on, guys. Thousands of years of art, and all anyone wanted to do was mimic the same styles that had existed since Ancient Greece.

That wasn't entirely fair. There were other artists who dabbled in abstract sculpture that sort of used contrast. At least they weren't terrified of angles.

But the trick was to use contrast *throughout* a piece and not as a simple geometric expression. Don't just bisect a rhombus with a triangle, *do* something with those shapes. *Say* something, damn it!

That was what Melissa did, and that was why she was on the cover of this month's issue of *Shape and Form* magazine.

At the moment, she was putting the finishing touches on a sculpture she entitled *Dilemma.* The sculpture was a massive bronze statue of a man's cranium with the skull opened to expose the brain. This sculpture was set within an asymmetrical ring of triangles, rhombuses and cylinders that jutted at odd angles over the brain. It was her most ambitious piece to date and had taken her over a year to complete.

But it was done, and it was beautiful. She took a step back and admired her work. "Raphael, eat your heart out."

She laughed at that. Raphael probably *would* eat his heart out if he saw that. He was the prettiest of all the "pretty" sculptors, and if he saw that horrific mess of shapes and protrusions over an exposed brain, he would… well, eat his heart out.

"Times change, buddy boy," Melissa said.

She giggled at her irreverence and danced over to the refrigerator she kept in the studio. She always felt giddy when she completed a piece, and since completing this piece had taken so much of her time that it had torpedoed her latest relationship, she had no reason to go home tonight.

So, she would celebrate by getting as plastered as she possibly could.

"Woo hoo! Champagne time!"

She popped the cork of a seventeen-year-old Dom Perignon that the director of the Museum of Fine Art in Chicago had given her and leaned back, gulping an obscene amount of the alcohol before taking it from her lips.

She laughed again and danced around the studio, feeling as free as a bird.

She didn't notice the shadow until it was too late. She heard a scraping noise and turned around to see one of her earlier works—a marble statue of a geisha holding a cobra up to her lips for a kiss—hurtling toward her.

Her last thought was, *You're going to kill me with* that *statue?*

CHAPTER ONE

Faith strained against her bonds, but they were expertly fastened, and she didn't budge. She tried to throw her weight from side to side, but the chair was bolted into the floor, and remained as unmoving as the rest of her.

Panic rose in her throat, but she took deep breaths to calm herself. She wouldn't get anywhere by giving into fear.

She looked around and took stock of her surroundings. The only light came from a crack in the wall behind her near the roof, but it illuminated enough to show her that she was in an old barn. It appeared to be abandoned. There were a few rusted old tools and a jumbled mess of metal that looked like it used to be a plow. Other than that, the only features she could see were herself and a surgical tray about three yards distant. On top of that tray was an array of instruments: scalpels, scissors, knives and saws, all pitted with rust and stained with dried blood.

Panic leapt to her throat again, and she did more breathing exercises to calm herself.

It was okay. They were looking for her. They knew that she had gone after the Donkey Killer. They would send people after her, and they would find her. It would be all right.

A sliver of light directly ahead speared her vision. The barn door opened slowly, its creaks reverberating through the barn like the groans of a dying animal. A shadow passed through the door, and then the light disappeared as the door closed.

Faith blinked her eyes to get them to adjust to the darkness again. She hoped desperately that when it did, she would see the face of her partner, Special Agent Michael Prince, telling her that they had caught the Donkey Killer, and he was going to cut her loose.

The voice that spoke instead dispelled every trace of that hope.

"Well, well, look who we have here."

The voice was a lilting, tremulous tenor that was incongruously high-pitched and soft for the man it belonged to.

That man stepped into the light and Faith felt a chill run through her spine as she stared into the insane eyes of Jethro Trammell, the Donkey Killer.

The nearly seven-foot-tall Trammell laughed lightly when he saw Faith's expression. "I'm so glad you came to visit me," he said, "I think we're going to have a lot of fun together."

I won't scream, *Faith promised herself.* I won't give him that satisfaction.

Trammell walked to the tray and cocked his head as he perused the tools available to him. After a moment, he selected a long, thin knife with a serrated edge.

He turned to Faith, and her breathing quickened as he walked closer. When he reached her, he knelt down and pressed the blade against her ear, drawing it lightly down her throat to her breast, her navel, and her thigh before finally bringing it to rest behind her right knee.

He leaned in close, and her nostrils flared at his sour breath.

"Let's see how you bleed, little girl."

He pressed the knife into her flesh, and Faith's willpower evaporated.

She screamed.

***

Faith woke with a gasp and sat bolt upright in her bed. Sweat poured from her forehead, and she knew without looking that the sheet underneath her would be damp with it as well.

The bed creaked, and a moment later a big, furry shape forced itself underneath her arm and began licking her face. She smiled softly and endured the kisses for a few seconds before gently pushing the dog away.

"Hey, Turk," she said. "It's okay. I'm all right. Just another nightmare."

The big German Shepherd who had been Faith's K9 partner for the past two years and change sat back and fixed her with a knowing look.

"I know, I know. It's been getting worse. Hey, at least David isn't here this time."

David Friedman was Faith's boyfriend and Turk's vet. The last time Faith had a nightmare, she had woken him up and then had to spend the rest of the night reassuring him that she was fine, and he didn't need to worry about her.

The problem was that she wasn't fine. She had gone months without a nightmare and even believed that she might have finally recovered from the trauma she suffered at Trammell's hands. Lately, though, the nightmares had returned. Four of the past five nights, Faith had woken in the middle of the night, drenched in sweat.

Make that five of the past six.

She sighed and rolled out of bed then headed to the shower. Trying to sleep after these nightmares was pointless. She was going to have to deal with waking up at—she checked her phone—three-twenty-five.

She sighed again and started the water, leaving it cold. The jet of icy water shocked her even further into wakefulness, but it also stopped the sweating and shaking.

She leaned forward against the wall of the shower and closed her eyes, allowing the water to flow over her and drive away the memory of the serial killer who had nearly claimed her for his own. That only brought the memory of the current killer after her to the forefront of her mind.

Jethro Trammell had killed seven victims in that barn before Faith's partner Michael burst in at the last second to save her from being victim number eight. Indirectly, though, he was responsible for thirty-two other victims because he had inspired someone else to take up his mantle.

That man was Franklin West, known to the FBI's Philadelphia Field Office as—appropriately—the Copycat Donkey Killer or just the Copycat Killer.

Faith had met West when he posed as a psychologist assigned to her by the FBI to help her cope with the trauma she suffered at the first Donkey Killer's hands. Faith prided herself on her ability to read people and tell when they were lying or withholding information, but she had somehow managed to spend five months without ever guessing that the man she was spilling all of her most personal secrets to was the man responsible for nearly five times as many deaths as his idol.

The killing had mostly stopped since Faith had exposed him and forced him into hiding, with two glaring exceptions in the form of her friend and mentor in the FBI, Supervisory Special Agent Gordon Clark, and Staff Sergeant James Decker, an old flame from the Marine Corps West killed for no other reason than to get her attention.

After those killings, the FBI had finally gotten its sugar-honey-iced-tea together and begun pursuing West in earnest. For several months, he had been incognito.

Then he had nearly beaten David to death and a few weeks later broke into Faith's apartment and attacked Turk. A month after that, he had hired a criminal to attack Turk in the animal hospital while Turk was recovering from injuries sustained in another investigation.

That attack had occurred three weeks ago. In the intervening weeks, Faith had been attacked four times, twice on the street, once in her apartment and once on the front steps of her job at the FBI field office in Philadelphia. All four of the men who attacked her claimed to have been hired by a man who matched West's description.

All four attacks were easily stopped. The people who attacked her were petty crooks with no experience tangling with an experienced FBI field agent who routinely dealt with violent serial killers and had a Marine Corps background to boot.

Not that Faith had to do much work. Once they saw Turk, the criminals—not surprisingly—became very compliant.

But throw enough spaghetti at a wall, and it would stick eventually. One of these crooks would fire a lucky shot, or Faith would slip and give them an opening, or West would hire someone who wasn't utterly incompetent.

Or West himself would come back. She and Turk had gotten the better of him the last time they encountered him, but the previous two times he had beaten both of them badly. They had only survived because West allowed them to.

I'm going to break you, Faith.

She shut the water off and left the shower. It was four o'clock by the time she was dressed in sweatpants and a t-shirt. Normally when she woke early, she would take Turk for a run, but after the last attack, she preferred to stay home where she could at least have some control of the environment.

She glanced at her front door and frowned slightly. It looked like a prison cell. Twin steel bars lined the top and bottom of the door, joined by a diagonal bar. To leave, Faith had to press a button that would retract the bars slightly and allow the door to open.

After she disabled the electronic deadbolt and unlocked the knob.

She sighed. She hated living like she was afraid. She wasn't even that afraid, not really. She was just…

"Tired. I'm tired of this."

Turk whined softly, and she smiled at him. "It'll be okay, boy. They'll get him eventually, and then we'll be able to rest."

She felt a touch of frustration that she still had to rely on others to catch West, but it dissipated quickly. When she was handling West's case, she only got herself and others into more trouble. Part of her still felt that she was the best person to be looking for West, but experience hadn't borne that out.

So, she would wait. At least for now.

"You want to see what's on tv, boy?" she said. "Here, come sit with me."

Turk joined her on the couch, putting his head on her lap and looking tenderly up at her. He would sit there, sometimes for hours, until he knew that Faith was feeling better.

We really don't deserve dogs, she thought as she ruffled his fur.

"Five more months, and then you get to rest, at least."

Turk was eight years and seven months old. By policy, all FBI K9s retired at the age of nine years old. Turk would reach that age soon, and when he did, Faith had already decided she wouldn't protest the decision. Strictly speaking, what would happen when he retired is that he would be placed for adoption, and Faith would be assigned another K9, but that wouldn't happen. She couldn't bear the thought of having another dog, and she couldn't bear the thought of someone else taking Turk.

The original plan was to retire when he did and move somewhere in the Midwest where she could work on cars and take Turk on adventures for the rest of his life. Safe adventures, the kind where homicidal maniacs weren't trying to kill them every few weeks.

She still hoped to do that, but hope was fading fast. West was still out there, and if he was still out there when Turk retired, there was no way Faith was moving away and no way she was retiring. At least now, she could keep abreast of progress on the case, and she lived in close proximity to dozens of very determined, very armed Special agents who would race each other to reach West first if she needed their help.

So the other option was to keep Turk here but keep her job. The problem with that was that Turk would end up cooped in a one-bedroom apartment for days on end, vulnerable to whoever managed to get in. Faith wouldn't be able to focus on work knowing that Turk was in danger at home, so she would end up getting people killed.

She could retire and stay here, she supposed. But if she did that, then she would never stop looking over her shoulder.

"There's no way out," she said softly. "Damn it, there's no way out."

Her phone rang. The Boss. She sighed with relief and answered.

"Bold, I need you at headquarters," the Boss said. "You have a case."

"On my way."

She hung up and grinned at Turk. A chance to get away for a bit was just what she needed.

"Come on, Turk. Let's go catch a bad guy."

CHAPTER TWO

Special Agent-in-Charge Grant Monroe was, in his day, the most decorated field agent in the FBI. He occupied a position much like Faith's own as the idol of all young agents and the favorite of FBI leadership. When he finally retired from the field and accepted the SAC position at the Philadelphia Field Office, those in the know predicted that he would make Deputy Director in ten years and Director in fifteen.

Unfortunately—or maybe fortunately—he got into a very public disagreement with then Deputy Director Smythe over a policy question related to the conduct of one of his agents. He got his way with the policy question but also ensured that he would spend the rest of his career in the same position.

And he didn't seem to mind one bit.

Known affectionately among the agents and analysts of the Philadelphia Field Office as the Boss, Monroe had the gruff bearing and no-nonsense attitude of a Marine Corps drill sergeant. Given that Faith was once a Marine herself, it made sense that she was one of his favorites.

Given that Michael grew up in a well-to-do family in Palo Alto, it made sense that he was one of the Boss's biggest annoyances.

"Morning, Boss," Michael said as he walked into the Boss's office. "Looking especially distinguished today. Did you dye your hair grayer?"

"Real funny, Prince," the Boss snapped. "There a reason you're ten minutes late?"

Michael blinked. "Ten minutes late? You only called me fifteen minutes ago."

"It takes five minutes to drive here from your house."

"I thought maybe you'd appreciate it if I was wearing pants."

Faith looked down and bit her lip to stifle a chuckle. The Boss glared at Michael a moment longer, then said, "Have a seat."

Michael sat next to Faith and frowned at her. "What are you doing here?"

"Working," she said. "What does it look like?"

Michael's brow furrowed. "Boss, she's been attacked four times in the past month. Why is she still here?"

"You can bitch about that later," the Boss said in a tone that indicated he wasn't interested in further conversation. He dropped a file in front of them and said, "Marissa Stone, twenty-nine, crushed to death by a marble statue."

"I'm sorry, what?" Michael said.

The Boss ignored him. "She was in her studio working late on a Memorial Day exhibit for the Chicago Museum of Modern Art. She was found the following night when police performed a wellness check after she refused to answer phone calls."

Faith opened the file and grimaced. Yep. She was crushed, all right.

"Damn," Michael whispered, shaking his head. "Family notified?"

"That she's dead? Yes. How she died? I hope not."

"Me too," Michael said.

"Not that I'm trying to put us out of work here," Faith said, "but are we sure this wasn't an accident?"

"There were marks on the door that indicate forced entry," the Boss said. "It looks like the killer forced the lock open but managed not to damage it so badly that he couldn't lock it again. They found a partial fingerprint too, no matches but it didn't belong to the victim."

"How could they tell?" Michael asked.

"Her right hand and left fingertips avoided being crushed."

"Got it."

"So they think someone lay in wait and pushed the statue onto her?" Faith asked.

"That's what it looks like."

"Okay. Again, not trying to put us out of work, but with only one murder, this should be a police case, not ours, right?"

"It would be, except that we were requested personally by Marissa's father."

"Who's Marissa's father?"

"The Ambassador to Germany and a personal friend of the President's. And before you ask, no, he's not a suspect. He was busy trying to convince the German Chancellor to approve sanctions against China when his daughter died."

"Got it. So we're doing this as a favor."

"That a problem, Bold?"

"No, not at all."

"Good. Then you two are on the first flight to Chicago."

“Hold on,” Michael said. “Faith should be in protective custody, not out in the open.”

Faith frowned at him. “I’m perfectly fine helping you, Michael.”

Michael sighed. “Faith, we’ve had this argument before.”

“Which makes it a little irritating that we have to have it again.”

“You’re being attacked weekly by assholes hired by a serial killer! You should be focusing on that, not running around chasing *more* bad guys.”

“That conversation is not up for reconsideration,” the Boss said coldly. “Bold—and you—are not and will never be part of the West case.”

“I don’t mean she should be part of the case, I mean she should be somewhere safe with massive former football players guarding her everywhere she doesn’t go because she’s not going anywhere until West is dead or in custody.”

“Michael, don’t speak for me!” Faith snapped. “I want to work. I’m not going to sit cooped up in my apartment all day just because West is throwing a tantrum about not being able to get to me.”

“What happens when he *does* get to you?”

“He stops becoming a problem, and I thank God that the FBI has such incredible lawyers.”

“I’m going to pretend I didn’t hear that,” the Boss said, “and I’m not going to hear anything else. Prince, Bold is on the case. End of story. Your flight leaves in an hour, get the hell out of my office.”

Michael frowned, but even he knew better than to push the boss any further. He stood and glared at Faith, then left the room.

Faith and Turk followed. Michael, as always, stopped by the break room for coffee before they left. When the door closed behind them, Faith crossed her arms and frowned. “What the hell was that?”

“That was your friend being concerned for your safety.”

“That was you overstepping your bounds in a big way. You don’t get to tell me how to protect myself.”

“I get to express displeasure when you choose not to protect yourself.”

"Oh, for God's sake, Michael. I have a Turk. I have a gun. I have my apartment protected by a deadbolt that only activates when I use my phone or get my eyes scanned. I have a massive steal beam that looks like it could stop a truck, and I have bulletproof glass in my windows."

“You have bulletproof windows?”

“Well, no, but you get the point.”

"I'd love to have bulletproof windows."

"Stop trying to distract me. Trust me, the best thing for me to do right now is work. I've been attacked four times while I've been here at home sitting still doing nothing. This is a chance to be thousands of miles from home working closely with you and the Chicago Police Department staying in a hotel with security cameras and panic buttons that lead straight to said police department. This is as safe a situation as I can possibly be in."

"I still like the idea of former football players with shotguns in a house in the middle of the Witness Protection neighborhood in Topeka."

"They have a neighborhood in Topeka?"

"No idea. I was just making a point."

He frowned irritably, but his shoulders weren't so tense anymore, and Faith could tell he was weakening. "Come on. You can tell me all about how irresponsible I'm being on the way to the airport."

He glared at her. "You're really annoying sometimes, you know that?"

"Yep. Sure do."

He rolled his eyes and followed her and Turk outside. Turk trotted eagerly next to Faith, happy to finally be outside after spending most of the past week indoors.

"Glad he's excited," Michael griped. "Ellie was going to make red velvet cheesecake for our anniversary dessert."

Faith laughed. "You're such an old man now."

"Why?"

"You're beautiful, adoring wife is about to enjoy her first wedding anniversary with you, and you're excited for the cheesecake?"

"Hey, we have sex all the time. Red velvet cheesecake is special."

Faith winced. "That's my fault. I did that to myself."

"Don't step in shit if you don't want to get dirty."

She gave him a strange look, and he shrugged. "Am I wrong?"

She rolled her eyes. "Drink your coffee. I'll drive."

She pulled out her keys, and Michael closed his hand over hers. "Not a chance in hell. *I'll* drive."

She chuckled and put her keys back in her pocket. "Whatever you say, old man."

Faith drove a 1999 Ford Crown Victoria Police Interceptor that was as heavy and powerful as it sounded. It was also a twenty-five-year-old body-on-frame sedan with the stock cloth seats and a well-maintained but very high-mileage engine. Faith loved the vibrations and rattles, and she didn't mind the fact that it liked to sway around corners and bounce over potholes, but Michael preferred to travel in style. His car was a late-model Grand Wagoneer with air suspension and massaging leather seats that he drove like a grandpa.

To each their own.

He *did* drink his coffee as they drove, at least. As they put distance between themselves and the Field office, Faith's excitement grew. She felt the usual fleeting sense of guilt at that excitement—a woman had died after all—but it didn't stifle her excitement.

"How's David?" Michael asked after a few minutes.

"He's good. We had dinner before he flew out for the conference. He seemed really excited."

"That's good. He's speaking at it this time, right?"

"He's introducing the keynote speaker."

"Oh. Well, that's a step up, right?"

She shrugged. "I guess. I don't know how the veterinary aristocracy works. I only know that he seemed excited to go."

"When are you two going to stop screwing around and get married already."

She sighed. There it was. "Someday. Maybe."

"That's what you said last time."

"Weird that my answer didn't change within the past week."

"I'm just saying. You guys have been dating a while now, you clearly love each other, you seem happier than I've seen you in years, Turk likes him—"

"I'm being targeted by a prolific and psychopathic serial killer who nearly killed him once already."

He sighed. "Yeah. There's that."

"It's a pretty big 'that,' Michael."

"I know. I'm not arguing with you."

"Once West is dealt with, I'll have more options," she explained. "I can figure out exactly what I want to do and plan a future. Right now, with so many unknowns, it makes more sense to just take things one day at a time."

"I got you. I was just asking."

"How's Ellie?"

"Beautiful and adoring. Also very upset that she won't get to make me red velvet cheesecake for our anniversary."

"Your anniversary's next week, right?"

"Yes."

"Well, don't lose hope. Maybe this will be one of those open and shut cases that only takes a few days to solve."

"Most of our cases only take a few days to solve."

"See? You're looking at the glass half full already."

Michael looked sideways at her. "You sound like her sometimes, you know that?"

Faith grimaced. "Don't tell her you said that."

Michael paused a moment, then said, "She doesn't hate you, you know."

Faith sighed. "Maybe not, but somehow I don't see us becoming best friends anytime soon."

When Faith first started investigating the Copycat Killer case, she had a minor mental break. During that mental break, she briefly suspected Ellie of being the killer. That, and an unfortunate incident when Turk decided he didn't like Ellie, had significantly chilled the relationship between the two women.

Michael didn't answer. They reached the airport a few minutes later, and when they finally lifted off, Faith felt another rush of excitement. She didn't think that her problems would disappear while she was away, but at least now she had something to focus on other than the madman who was after her.

CHAPTER THREE

Marissa Stone's studio was—like many artist's studios—a converted apartment. This particular apartment was on the tenth floor of a medium-rise apartment building near downtown. The Chicago police officer who met them there—a short, thickly built man who introduced himself as Detective Ricardo—led them upstairs.

"Glad you guys made it when you did. The super's been bugging me to release the room so they can clean it and start showing it again. Not sure how they figure on renting it out when they've got the stink of dead body filling the place, but hey, gotta give them props for hoping."

He opened the door and led them inside. Michael's eyes widened when he saw the sculptures. "How the hell did the floor not collapse underneath her?"

"I guess she paid for renovations to strengthen the room's frame so it could handle the extra weight."

"It would take more than just strengthening the room," Michael said. "There's got to be fifteen tons of marble and brass in here."

Ricardo shrugged. "That's just what we were told."

Faith was inclined to agree with Michael. Strengthening the room didn't seem like enough to handle the weight of the works she saw here. Maybe Marissa's father had paid to have the building remodeled.

Not that it really mattered. They were here to investigate the murder, not inspect the building.

"Maybe I'm just not that into art," Michael said, "but this is some weird stuff."

"I think avante-garde is the term artists prefer."

Michael pointed at a sculpture of a small man holding open a larger man's mouth so it stretched three times the length of the rest of its head while another man stood on a ladder and dumped a box of something labeled COMPLACENCY into the gaping maw. "This is avante-garde?"

"Hey, I'm not an artist either."

Most of the other sculptures were similarly odd. They couldn't really be said to have a common theme except that they all involved animals or people depicted in very unlifelike poses and dimensions.

Other than that, it seemed like the result of Marissa's drug-induced fevers.

Well, maybe it was. That worked for Van Gogh.

Faith frowned when she saw the statue that had killed Marissa lifted and the body gone. "When did you remove her body?"

"Last night."

"Why didn't you wait for us to look at the scene? You couldn't wait twelve hours?"

"Her family wanted her back. Her dad's friends with the President, I guess, so the chief called and personally arranged for her to be recovered. Not that there was much to recover. Fortunately, the family's going to have her cremated so they won't have to look at... well, you know."

Faith sighed. She wasn't happy at looking at a tampered-with crime scene, but there was nothing she could do about it now. "Show me where it happened."

Ricardo pointed to a large smear of red and brown on the floor about two yards to Faith's left. "That's not paint," he said.

Michael grimaced and turned away. Turk whined and shook his head. Faith managed to control her reaction a little better, but her stomach still turned. There were still chunks in the smear and on the statue sitting in front of it.

"I wouldn't get closer than that," Ricardo said. "I know the statue was pushed, but it's still fifteen hundred pounds of marble. One wrong move, and we end up scraping you off the floor."

Thanks for that image," Faith thought drily. "I was told there were signs of a break-in?"

"Yes." Ricardo gestured for her to follow and led her back to the doorway. He squatted down and shined his light on the jamb near the latch. "See those grooves there above the latch and those marks on the brass plate that holds the latch?"

Faith leaned close and saw the marks he was talking about. They were unmistakably marks from a tool used to defeat the lock. "Yeah, I see them."

"That's what clued me in. Then you come over here..."

He stood and walked behind another statue—this one a large brass image of an Aztec emperor bowing to what looked like a capuchin monkey—and shined his light on the floor. Faith could see scuff marks that looked like partial shoe prints.

"Not enough there to get anything usable," Ricardo said, "but enough to tell me that someone else was here the night she was murdered. Then you have the fingerprint we lifted off the statue and the fact that the statue slid backwards a few inches before it fell, and it all points to someone knocked it over onto Miss Sculptor of the Year."

Faith frowned. "There's no need to mock her, Detective."

"I'm not. She really was Sculptor of the Year."

He pointed to the coffee table, where a copy of an art magazine sat with an image of a young woman smiling on the cover.

"That's her?"

"That's her."

Faith picked up the magazine and got her first good look at Marissa Stone. She looked confident, a little arrogant, even. That could be a motive. Perhaps someone was jealous of her success and wanted to get her out of the way.

She set the magazine down and turned back to Ricardo. "Were you able to retrieve security footage from the building?"

He chuckled, a touch bitterly. "Camera's don't work. Haven't for years. Ever since that measure failed that would require them, you have a ton of buildings like this one with cameras installed to make it look like they care, but they never work. They're just more sculptures."

"And no one saw anything suspicious the night of the murder?"

"They all say no."

"They didn't hear anything?" Michael asked. "That's a big damn statue. Even if the room is reinforced to handle those kinds of falls, it would have made a noise or something."

"The guy downstairs was out of town visiting his grandfather. The woman next door said that sounds always came from Marissa's room. She wasn't known for working quietly. I guess that's hard to do when your job is to chisel marble and melt brass."

"So they heard a big boom, decided it was business as usual and didn't so much as knock on the door for two days to check on her?"

Ricardo met Michael's eyes. "I get that Philadelphia is the city of brotherly love, so maybe this is odd to you, but Chicago is the city of 'screw you and mind your own business.' Honestly, I'm more surprised that anyone bothered to call for a wellness check. Most of the time, when people living alone die, we don't get a call until the smell becomes unbearable."

"But she didn't live here," Faith interjected.

“No, she didn’t,” Ricardo confirmed. “She lived in a high-rise downtown. The Avanti. Nice building. Jake Gyllenhaal has a penthouse there supposedly or used to.”

“Did you interview anyone there?” Faith asked.

“Yep. Talked to the super, the manager, the neighbors, the ex.”

“Her ex lives there?”

“Not anymore, but we talked to him. They all said that she was behaving the way she usually did. No mood swings, sudden irritability or depression, no one new in her life—mysterious or otherwise. This came out of nowhere.”

“How was the ex when you talked to him?”

“Inconsolable. Blamed himself. Said he should have been more understanding and never should have left her, yadda yadda. Typical stuff.” He chuckled. “Kind of odd for him to be so bent out of shape considering his alibi was that he was in bed with another woman at the time of Marissa’s death.”

“Verified?”

“Oh yeah. Cameras actually work at his place. Marissa’s time of death is estimated at eleven-thirty-five p.m. Tuesday. Camera shows the ex getting home—new girl in tow—at eleven-oh-eight, and the lovebirds don’t leave the room until nine-forty-five.”

“Alibis all around,” Michael said. “Well, no one said this would be easy.”

“It would have to be someone who knew where she worked,” Faith said. “So they would have to be somewhat close to her.”

Ricardo chuckled. “She’s on the cover of a magazine. I’m not an artiste by any means, but if she’s renowned enough to be on the cover of a magazine, it’s a good bet that a lot of people knew where she worked.”

“Well, let’s get a list of that ‘lot of people,’” Faith said, “and get people talking to them.”

"Will do. Before I get started on that, anything else you guys need?"

“Keep the media off our backs,” Michael said. “I’d rather not deal with crowds of reporters at the moment.”

Ricardo shrugged. “I’ll do my best. Can’t guarantee that I’ll hold them off for long, though. Right now, the family wants the media circus kept to a minimum, but if we don’t give them results soon, they’re going to get all self-righteous. You know how it is.”

Unfortunately, the FBI agents did. “Thank you, Detective,” Faith said. “Keep me posted if you hear anything.”

"I will."

He left the room, and Michael asked, "You don't want to go talk to the ex and the neighbors? Maybe see if there's anything Detective wishes-he-was-from-Brooklyn missed?"

She shook her head. "No, I don't think this was a crime of passion or a case of angry neighbors. I'm still leaning toward jealous fellow artist."

"Does that stuff really happen?" Michael asked.

"Why not? We've worked stranger cases."

"I know, it just seems… I don't know. Cheesy. Like a late-night pulp mystery."

Faith smiled slightly. "You watch a lot of late-night pulp mysteries?"

"Sure. Ellie's in bed by nine o'clock most nights, so I stay up and watch old tv shows until I fall asleep."

She laughed. "Oh my God, you *are* an old man."

He rolled his eyes. "Hey Turk, you find anything interesting? Anything that can rescue me from this conversation?"

Turk shook his head and snorted irritably. He trotted over to Faith, who reached down and scratched him behind his ears. "That's okay," she said. "We'll find something." She stood and walked back over to the statue. "Whether it's a jealous artist or not, this was personal. Someone waited here for her to come home, then waited for God knows how long for her to stand in just the right spot for them to tip the statue over onto her."

"Maybe it wasn't personal. Maybe the killer was just a coward."

Faith shook her head. "Marissa was five-foot-two and a hundred and eight pounds. Whoever killed her was strong enough to tip a fifteen-hundred-pound statue over. I know it takes a lot less force to tip a statue over than it does to lift it, but I don't see anyone smaller than Marissa being able to do it."

"It's not just about beating her in a fight. The neighbors were used to the sound of sculpting work, but I'll bet they weren't used to the sound of a woman screaming for her life."

"Good point."

They stood in silence for a moment. Faith tried to picture the scene in her head.

The killer shows up. He or she is nervous, whether they let it show or not. They pick the lock on the door, which takes them a moment since they scrape grooves in the wood and brass before they get to the lock. The door opens, and they think to close and lock it again so they don't raise Marissa's suspicions.

Then they probably look around the studio. Either they've been here before, and they already know how they want to kill Marissa, or they take a moment to figure out a plan. The plan ends up being crush her to death, gruesome but brutally intelligent since it leaves very little evidence behind for the police to look through. What evidence could be left behind they apparently take care to avoid leaving.

That being said, they did leave a partial fingerprint. So they don't think to bring gloves, but probably realize that mistake and cover their hands with their sleeves. One finger slips out when they do the deed, hence the partial.

So they wait. Marissa gets home, works for a while, then makes it over to the statue at some point. Crash bang boom, statue falls on her. Killer probably doesn't linger but gets out of Dodge ASAP. It's a busy building, but it's also late at night. Someone should have seen something. She doesn't buy the "screw you and mind your own business" line.

Faith's phone rang, pulling her out of her thoughts. She pulled it out of her pocket and frowned. Ricardo already.

"Bold. You forget something?"

"No, unfortunately not. We have a new crime scene."

Faith's eyes widened. "Another person killed by a statue?"

"No, but another break-in that looks a hell of a lot like that one."

Faith's lips set in a grim line. "All right. We're on our way."

CHAPTER FOUR

There was a body for them to look at this time. It was in better condition than Faith imagined Marissa's was, but short of being crushed to death, this was about as gruesome a way to die as Faith could imagine.

"Name's Cassandra Holt," Ricardo offered. "Thirty-two. Ran this bakery for the past ten years. Specialized in vegan offerings and sustainably sourced ingredients. You know, the typical trendy stuff."

"I'm guessing the ingredient that did that wasn't sustainably sourced," Michael said drily.

Cassandra lay in a pool of blood-laced vomit. Her body was arched and stiff, and her eyes and mouth were open wide in a rictus of terror. Her throat was scratched where she had clawed at it in the moments before her death. Next to her mouth, the second half of the muffin that had killed her lay soaked in bile.

"No, I can't imagine it was," Ricardo replied. "We'll have to wait for toxicology to figure out exactly what killed her, but my first guess is a plant-based alkaloid like strychnine or atropine."

Turk sniffed the body and whined mournfully.

Michael shook his head. "God. This killer's a sicko."

"It's too early for me to be confident that it's the same person who killed Marissa Stone," Ricardo said. "Break-ins happen all the time, and the signs we saw aren't necessarily indicative that it's the same person. But, as they say, if you hear hoofbeats, you don't think zebras."

"So let's see the hoofbeats," Faith said.

Ricardo led the two of them to the door and shined his light near the jamb. Again, Faith saw the telltale grooves and marks on the latch that indicated the lock was forced.

"There's nowhere to hide this time, though," Faith said, "and the poison came from the muffin, right?"

"That's the hypothesis. We'll need the coroner's report to be sure."

"There's no sign of a struggle," Michael said. "Except for her death throes. I think Faith is right. The killer got in, so the killer would have to get out."

"Any reason why he couldn't get out the same way?" Ricardo asked.

"He wouldn't be able to lock the door after," Michael said. "That would leave the situation suspicious."

Ricardo's eyes narrowed. "Hmm. Hey Marco!"

A tall young man in a corporal's uniform looked up from where he was taping off the scene.

"Check the windows and the back door and see if you can find any sign of our killer. We think he left a different way than he came in."

"Are we sure it's a he?" Faith asked.

"Hell, I'm not sure of anything right now," Ricardo said, "but it's usually a he."

"I thought poison was more of a she thing," Michael opined.

"It is, but crushing someone with a three-quarter ton statue is definitely a he thing."

"Fair enough."

Marco returned from the back door. "Door's unlocked," he told Ricardo. "I'll send some men out to see if we can find anything."

"Take my K9," Faith said. "Turk, go with them."

Turk barked and trotted after Marco. Faith walked behind the counter and looked at the scene more closely.

"This is interesting. It looks like this was the only pastry she ate. I see a dozen bins here, but only one of them open and only one muffin missing from it."

"Staged, maybe?" Michael asked. "To make it look like it was a bad muffin?"

Faith shook her head. "No muffin's that bad. I think the killer knew that she would pick that specific muffin."

"But why? What's special about it?"

"I don't know," Faith said. "I might be overthinking it. It's possible he poisoned the whole batch."

"I'll take them to the lab," Ricardo said. "We'll run a tox screen on it and figure out if there's anything fishy. Better label it as evidence now, though, or the officers might get the wrong idea."

He took the box from Faith and pulled a marker from his pocket. While he was marking it, Faith and Michael brainstormed.

"So we have two very different causes of death," Faith said, "but the same method of entry."

"We'll have to find out if the victims knew each other," Michael said. "It's possible that they had a mutual friend who went off the deep end."

"You know, very few people just go off the deep end," Faith observed. "Most of the ones in the deep end swim there their entire lives. We just don't see them until they pull someone else under."

"Well put," Michael said.

"That's me," Faith said drily, "the serial killer whisperer."

"So let's assume for the sake of argument that they don't know each other," Michael said, "what other pattern do we see?"

Faith cocked her head. "It could be some kind of statement. The sculptor crushed to death by her statue, the baker poisoned by her own bread."

"Hell of a way to make a statement. And what kind of statement would that be, anyway? Don't pursue your dream? Don't be talented and successful?"

"Could be someone who's jealous. Maybe someone who never succeeded and resented watching everyone else succeed."

"But who's everyone else?" Michael shook his head. "I really feel that our killer knew both victims. Even if the victims didn't know each other, even if they didn't know him, he knew them."

"So how does he know a sculptor and a baker from two opposite sides of Chicago at the same time without them knowing him?"

"That's a question we'll have to answer."

They heard excited barking from the back and quickly headed behind the bakery. Turk was barking at a dumpster about twenty yards from the back door.

Faith and Michael quickly caught up to him. Marco drew his weapon and said, "If anyone's hiding in that dumpster, you better come out now with your hands where I can see them, or I will shoot you, understand?"

No one answered. Marco repeated his warning, then nodded at the other officer standing next to him. The other officer pushed open the dumpster and shone his light into the bin. "No one here," he said.

Turk continued to bark, and Marco said, "Well, something's in there. The dog's going crazy."

"This thing's piled high with trash," the officer said. "We can search through it, but it's going to be… hold on."

He peered more closely into the bin, and after a second, he said, "I got a needle. Here, let me—"

"Whoa!" Detective Ricardo called. Faith turned to see him jogging toward them, his hand upraised. "Hold on a moment there, Guillermo. Don't *ever* grab a needle with your bare hands. Especially when we're ninety percent certain that needle contained a poison that did *that."* He hooked a thumb back at the bakery. "Put some gloves on. Thick ones. And grab the syringe by the fat end."

Guillermo complied and gingerly retrieved the needle. Turk barked excitedly when Guillermo removed it, and Faith ruffled his fur. "Good boy. Good job, Turk."

Ricardo opened an evidence bag and Guillermo carefully dropped the needle into the bag. "Beautiful. Ladies and gentlemen, pedantry requires me to say we can't be sure until we get this tested, but barring something shocking, we have our murder weapon!" He looked at Faith and Michael and said, "We'll get that dusted for prints too. Hopefully we get lucky and stop this guy before he gets someone else."

"So we're sure it's the same guy?" Marco asked.

"It's starting to look that way," Faith said.

"But why? What kind of enemies could a sculptor and a baker have?"

"I hate to be the guy to say it," Ricardo offered, "but it could just be that they're women."

"Jilted lover?" Michael asked.

"Could be. Could also be one of those incel types."

Faith shook her head. "No, 'incel' types like attention. They're the ones who shoot up crowded places, not the ones who sneak around and hide. They want to get caught. Our killer *definitely* doesn't want to get caught."

"He should have taken his needle home with him then," Ricardo said. "All right boys. Let's turn this over to CSI. Marco, Guillermo, hang out here until they're finished. I'm going to get the evidence back to the lab and light a fire under their asses."

Faith, Michael and Turk headed for the hotel they would stay at while they were in Chicago. They drove in silence for a while, both ruminating on the scenes they had witnessed.

Michael broke the silence. "I gotta wonder what was going through this guy's head. The first scene I understood. I mean, I didn't, but I did. He wants to literally crush Marissa's dreams. He wants her wiped off the face of the Earth. He wants to see her destroyed. I can even understand the patience in that scenario."

"He wanted it to be the perfect killing," Faith agreed.

"He wanted to *see* the perfect killing," Michael clarified. "At least, I thought he did. But this second one?" He shook his head. "Why go to all that trouble without even sticking around to make sure that your victim is dead? I get that maybe he knew that she really liked lemon poppyseed muffins, so she usually sneaked a cake or two, but what if she didn't? What if she sold the muffins and ended up killing a bunch of kids?"

"We don't know yet that the whole batch was compromised," Faith said. "He might have had reason to believe that she'd pick a specific muffin."

"Maybe. It's not really the part about killing kids that makes me wonder. It's the part about not being there to see it happen. Usually, when people kill other people this brutally, they get off on watching it. That's why most people who are strangled to death die facing their victims. It's the same reason arsonists usually stick around to watch their fires burn. Why stick poison into a muffin, then leave?"

Faith shook her head. "Normally, I'd have some astute observation to offer you, but I'm coming up empty this time."

He sighed. "Well, it's day one. Considering that, we're doing well. We have an MO, a murder weapon, and probably the poison used for vic two. We'll consider that the silver lining to this cloud. You hungry?"

"I could eat."

"Perfect. We're getting deep dish."

Faith chuckled. "Of course we are."

"Hey, we're in Chicago. You can't go to Chicago without getting deep dish pizza."

"Well, order it delivery. I'm beat."

"Already? It's barely nine o'clock."

"I didn't sleep well last night."

"Nightmares?"

Faith tensed slightly. "Yeah."

He sighed. Faith waited for him to say something unhelpful about going somewhere safe and staying there until West was in custody, but he only said, "I'm sorry."

Her shoulders relaxed. "Me too."

"We'll get him," he promised. "Sooner or later, we'll get him."

"Yeah. I know."

They reached the hotel a few minutes later. The deep-dish pizza Michael ordered was very good, according to him, but Faith decided she preferred thin crust. The deep dish was delicious but too messy.

After dinner, she showered and then went to bed. She was exhausted, but her mind raced too much for her to fall asleep.

As she lay awake, she thought of their Marissa and Cassandra. Both of them happy. Both of them enjoying their life's dream. Both of them with a bright future ahead of them, only to have it swiftly and brutally taken by a coward who didn't even show his face to his victims.

You'll show your face to me. I'll see you. Then there will be nowhere for you to hide.

CHAPTER FIVE

Faith strained against her bonds, but they were expertly fastened, and she didn't budge. She tried to throw her weight from side to side, but the chair was bolted into the floor, and remained as unmoving as the rest of her.

She looked around and took stock of her surroundings. Light filtered in through a crack in the wall behind her, shedding soft light on the interior of what looked to be a barn.

Trammell's barn.

Panic rose in her throat, but she fought it down. She wouldn't get anywhere by giving into fear.

She looked ahead and saw a surgical tray topped with...

That wasn't right. There was only a single syringe on top of the tray. She frowned. That wasn't right. Trammell cut his victims, he didn't poison them.

"Well, well, well. Who do we have here?"

She froze. That voice definitely wasn't right. Gone was Trammell's tremulous lilt. In its place was a mellow, softspoken voice with a slight drawl.

"West," she whispered.

"That's what they call me," Franklin West said.

He stepped out of the shadows and smiled at Faith with the benign grin he used to wear when he pretended to be her psychologist. He wore the outfit he wore during their sessions, too, a brown wool vest over a long-sleeved white button-down above tan pants and brown Oxfords. His round-rimmed glasses made his eyes appear gentle and curious, but Faith could see the viciousness behind that façade.

He lifted the syringe and said, "You've been a very troublesome patient, Bold. We're going to give you a little something to calm you."

He depressed the tip of the syringe and a few droplets of liquid sprayed out. Faith's heart started to pound, and a cold sweat broke out on her forehead.

I won't scream, *she promised herself.* I won't give him that satisfaction.

West approached her, smiling down at her with the same benign, crazed grin. He knelt in front of her and held her head firmly with his left hand to keep her from moving. She could smell mint and cinnamon on his breath from the mints he ate compulsively during their sessions.

"This won't hurt a bit," he said gently, menacingly.

He pressed the syringe against her neck and—

***

Faith woke with a start. Michael pulled back and said, "Sorry. I didn't mean to startle you. It's almost nine o'clock."

"What?" She sat up and looked at her phone. The time showed eight-fifty-two. She sighed and threw the covers off. Turk jumped out of the way before they covered him. "Sorry, boy."

"Sorry," Michael said, "I would have woken you up earlier, but I figured you needed the sleep."

She sighed. "It's fine, but next time, if I'm still out by seven, wake me up. Is there coffee?"

"And breakfast. I grabbed a protein bar, an apple and a muffin. I took a bit out to make sure it wasn't poisoned."

She glared at him, and he lifted his hands apologetically. "Not funny. Got it."

"Any news from Ricardo?" she asked as she dressed.

"Actually, yes," he said. "That's why I woke you up. They got the results back from the lab."

"Already? That was fast."

"I guess he wasn't joking about lighting a fire under their asses."

"Always nice to have good help." She pulled her vest on and stepped into her shoes. "What do we have?"

"The muffins turned out to be fine. He really did guess exactly what muffin she would pick. Ricardo's guess is that it was the one closest to the tab that opened the lid on that container. He figures it would be the muffin most people would choose."

"Okay, well, that doesn't really help us."

"It tells us that our guy was careful to target Cassandra and Cassandra alone," Michael countered, "but I have bigger news: we have our poison."

"We do? Outstanding. What is it?"

"Anabasine."

"Anabasine? What's that?"

"Evidently, it's an ingredient in pesticides. It's not used often anymore because of its toxicity, but some people still purchase it for landscaping."

"That's good. That's big. I'm guessing this isn't something normal people could get."

"It's not something normal people would have a reason to get. So either our killer is going to be the odd man out who purchased a quart of this stuff, or he's going to be one of very few people in the Chicago area who use it professionally."

"Wonderful. Have Ricardo get a list of names. We'll start talking to people."

Michael grinned and held up his phone. On the phone was a picture of a Caucasian man in his mid-forties. "Gregory Marten," Michael said. "Forty-five. Has a landscaping business headquartered five miles from here. He's the only guy within ninety miles who purchases anabasine-based pesticides. And," he swiped left on his screen and the image changed to Marten's social media page, "he just *raves* about Cassandra's muffins."

"You don't say?"

"That's not all. His biggest customer? The Museum of Modern Art." He scrolled down a bit. "Here's a picture of him standing in front of a mural advertising the Museum's new exhibit. Guess who that is on the mural?"

"Marissa Stone."

"The very same."

"Damn," Faith said. "I really like Ricardo."

Michael rolled his eyes. "I do too, but this is *my* work, thank you very much."

"Oh." She reddened slightly. "Well, thank you."

"You're very welcome," he said pertly. "So, what do we think? Should we go have a convo with Mr. Marten?"

"I think that's an excellent idea."

***

The subscript under the sign for Old Glory Landscaping announced that they had been "Proudly serving patriots of the Greatest Nation on Earth since 2000." Above that subscript and the name of the business was an image of the American Flag flying over purple mountains and amber waves of grain.

“Majestic,” Michael commented.

He parked in the building’s parking lot—“Reserved for Patriots only”—and the three of them headed inside.

The interior of the building was just as brazen as the exterior. Banners depicting the coats of arms of each branch of the military covered the walls, and the front counter had a VA banner that read SUPPORT OUR TROOPS. Two American flags stood on either end of the room, and a figurine of the Statue of Liberty sat on the counter behind which stood their suspect.

Gregory Marten looked exactly like the kind of man who would own a business adorned with an excess of patriotic symbols. He stood six-foot-three and a comfortable two hundred forty pounds, most of which he carried in his arms and shoulders. His graying blonde hair was cropped in a crew cut and he wore a gray USMC t-shirt about three sizes too small for him above camo pants and steel-toed combat boots.

When he looked up and saw the FBI agents, he smiled and walked around the counter to greet them. “Welcome! Nice to welcome a couple of public servants into my business. I’m guessing my friends at Great Lakes referred you guys to me.”

“Actually, no,” Faith said. “We’re here to ask about Cassandra Holt?”

Marten’s brow furrowed. “Cassandra? As in Cassandra from Cassandra’s Muffin Shop?”

“Yes, sir.”

Marten grinned again. “Love her stuff. Have to say, I’m not big on the whole vegan thing. I think people were built to eat meat. Why else would we have evolved the ability to hunt? Have to say, though, those vegan muffins she makes are delicious! That’s what you get when you use good old American grains to make your food. She was a big supporter of the troops, too. She did a whole Veterans Day thing last year. Baked muffins, cakes, pastries and all sorts of stuff with veteran themes.” His brow furrowed again. “Why are you coming to me about her?”

“She was found dead in her bakery last night.” Faith informed him.

Marten blinked. “Dead?”

“Yes, sir. May we speak to you for a few minutes?”

He frowned slightly. “Why me? I mean… she’s dead? What happened?”

“We’ve answered question two,” Michael said. “We’ll be happy to answer questions one and three, but would you prefer to do this somewhere more private?”

Marten blinked again. “Uh yeah. Yeah, hold on a second.” He walked back behind his desk and picked up a phone. “Julie? Can you come watch the front desk for a minute? Thank you.”

He hung up and said, “Jesus. I was just there yesterday.”

“You don’t say?”

He scowled at Michael. “Morning. Yesterday morning.”

Michael lifted his hands. “Sure.”

The door to the EMPLOYEES ONLY area opened and a petite Vietnamese woman who Faith guessed to be around twenty-five smiled nervously at them. She looked at Marten and asked in a voice that wasn’t nearly as quiet as she thought it was, “Is everything okay?”

“Everything’s fine, Julie,” Marten replied, making no attempt to soften his voice. “I just need to speak to these two for a moment.”

Julie nodded and looked anxiously back at Faith and Michael. She relaxed slightly when she saw Turk. Faith followed her eyes and saw Turk smiling happily at Julie, his tail wagging back and forth without a sign of suspicion.

That wasn't necessarily a sign of innocence. Turk had been wrong before, not often, but enough that Faith knew he could be fooled if a criminal was careful enough. Still, he had never been wrong about aggression before. Marten might look imposing, but he was unlikely to try anything.

“Okay,” Marten said, “you two can follow me into my office.”

The two human agents—K9 companion in tow—followed Marten through the EMPLOYEES ONLY door. Considering the boldness of the décor in the front of the building, Faith was somewhat surprised to see a modestly appointed collection of offices with the standard issue beige paint and paneled desks.

Marten’s office was at the end of the hallway and was only slightly more well-appointed than those of his employees. The room was a little larger and the desk appeared to be of real wood rather than wood-paneling over particle board, but it was cheap pine wood, and the computer was a bargain unit that usually sold for three hundred dollars.

There was a slight return to the patriotic décor, however. The USMC flag stood next to yet another American flag behind Marten’s desk, and a small bookshelf was filled with titles by well-known former servicemen and women.

Marten sat behind his desk and gestured for Faith and Michael to take the two seats in front of it. When he spoke again, his voice was calmer and less gregarious.

"I assume I'm a suspect. That's why you two came to see me."

"Yes. She was poisoned with anabasine."

Marten's eyes widened. "Pure anabasine?"

"Yes. Care to offer an idea why?"

"Your killer works in a chem lab. Or stole from a chem lab. Or knows someone who works in a chem lab. We don't sell pure anabasine, and we don't purchase it either."

Brianna's brow furrowed. "You're the largest purchaser of anabasine in the Midwest."

"We're the largest purchaser of anabasine-based pesticide in the Midwest. We purchase the product from overseas."

"Where exactly?"

"Indonesia. You'd be surprised, but they have a very sophisticated chemical industry."

"Forgive me," Michael said, "but it seems odd that someone as patriotic as you would outsource your best-selling product."

"To clarify, our product is landscaping services and the pesticide is a tool we use for our services. But I understand your point. The reality is there are things some countries do that our country can't or won't do anymore. The environmentalists have a stranglehold on Congress, and they've crippled a lot of American industries and forced us to turn to foreigners to survive. But I don't think you're here to talk about my political beliefs or my perceived hypocrisy on that front."

"No," Faith agreed. "We're here to talk about Cassandra Holt. How well did you know her?"

"I didn't. She saw me once or twice a week when I would stop by for a muffin. Nice girl."

"Were you attracted to her?"

Marten smiled slightly, but Faith detected more annoyance than guilt or fear. "No. She was pretty, but she's not my type."

"What about Marissa Stone? You know her?"

"Who?"

Michael pulled up the image on his phone of Marten standing in front of the Chicago Museum of Modern Art banner depicting Marissa. "This girl."

"Oh, the sculptor? No, I don't know her. I'm not really an art guy. I like Ansel Adams. You know him?"

“I do,” Michael said. “My wife’s a big fan.”

“If you don’t know her, then why is there a picture of you standing next to a picture of her?” Faith asked.

“That’s a picture of me standing in front of my firm’s work. You’ll notice the banner is off to the side, and the girl—Miss Stone, I guess—is barely in the picture. This is a picture of me standing in front of a landscaping design making liberal use of mica-heavy granite stones, trimmed boxwood bushes and petunias, marigolds and poppies. In the winter, those plants will be dormant and the rows of polyanthus, camellia and calendula. The idea was to show how as some life dies, other life emerges.”

“Very artistic for a guy who isn’t into art,” Michael observed.

“It wasn’t my idea. It was the museum’s idea. They hired me to perform the work because I was the only firm who could handle the order within the schedule provided.”

“Why include Marissa’s image in the picture?”

He gave Faith a knowing look. “Do you want the politically correct answer or the honest one?”

“The honest one.”

"She's hot. Sex sells, and while there are fortunately some who would consider me sexy, most people would rather look at a pretty girl with a nice smile and a good figure than me. I put that up on the website, knowing people would see it. The caption is supposed to direct their eyes to the landscaping work. I guess it didn't work for you guys."

“Was Marissa your type?” Michael asked.

“No. I like Korean women. I always have. When I was in elementary school, I was picked on a lot, but the Korean girl next door would always play with me and make me feel better. She came to every one of my birthday parties until her family moved away when I was in fifth grade. We still talk occasionally. I’ve been hooked on Korean girls ever since.”

Faith and Michael shared a look and decided not to pursue the subject further.

“So you wouldn’t have a reason to crush Marissa to death with a statue?” Faith asked.

Marten laughed. “No. No reason to do that.” When he saw the agents’ serious faces, his smile faded. “Oh Christ, you’re serious. I just assumed she was poisoned like Cassandra.”

“Can you tell me your whereabouts three nights ago as well as last night?”

“I was with Julie. She and I have been dating for the past six months. We don’t broadcast it since she’s an employee, but she and I have been getting serious. Three nights ago, we were at Lake Itasca. We got back the next morning. I can show you our ticket stubs, and the airline can confirm we were there. Last night, we were at home—my home. Julie can confirm I was with her, but we don’t have any third-party verification for that.”

“We’ll follow up,” Faith said. “Thank you.”

Michael called the airline while Faith spoke with Julie. Julie was clearly embarrassed, but she confirmed that the two of them were in a relationship and that Marten was with her the night before. The airline corroborated Marten’s story, and the two agents found themselves once more at square one.

They returned to the office to give Marten the good news—well, good for him, anyway. He nodded and said, “For what it’s worth, I really hope you find this guy. I didn’t know Marissa, but Cassandra was a good girl. She didn’t deserve this.”

“Neither of them did,” Faith agreed. “Thank you for your time.”

When the three of them left the building, Michael griped, “Well, that was a waste of time.”

“Not necessarily,” Faith said. “We have a connection between the victims.”

“What connection? A landscaper we’ve now proven innocent?”

“Support for the military. Marissa was completing a project for the Memorial Day exhibit. Cassandra had a line of veterans-themed baked goods.”

“Marissa’s project had nothing to do with soldiers or veterans, though. It was a statue of a guy’s brain with shapes hanging over it.”

“It’s a thin connection,” Faith admitted, “but we’ve seen killers make thinner connections.”

Michael shook his head. “There was no reason. This guy just wanted to find a reason to kill her.”

Faith wondered why it was that even the most violent among them looked for excuses to justify their actions. How was it that people’s consciences could see nothing wrong with brutally killing people yet still feel a need to rationalize it?

Maybe at the end of the day, civilization was just the mask humanity wore to hide the fact that they were still little more than violent animals.

CHAPTER SIX

Getting to Marissa's family proved to be difficult. Her parents were still overseas, and the assistant they spoke to said that their schedule likely wouldn't open up for weeks.

"They're not coming to the funeral?"

"The talks are at a crucial juncture. I'm afraid the ambassador can't spare the time."

"Not even to attend his daughter's funeral?"

The assistant paused a moment, then said in a quieter voice. "Believe me, he would if he could. But his job means he has to make sacrifices sometimes. They'll hold another memorial when he's able to return home, but… well, let's just say I'm glad I don't have his job."

"Me too," Faith agreed. "Poor guy. Well, have him call as soon as he can."

"I will."

With Marissa's family unavailable, they decided to focus on Cassandra's family first. The Holts, thankfully, lived in Zion, an hour north of the city and were involved in work that didn't require them to sacrifice everything for the sake of the job.

They didn't have to go to Zion, though. The family had been notified of her death upon completion of the autopsy that morning and were currently at Ricardo's precinct talking with detectives. The agents arrived around lunchtime and got Ricardo's blessing to speak to them.

"The dad's gonna be a little more helpful," he advised. "Mom's in bad shape right now."

"Understandably," Faith replied. "We'll talk to Dad, then."

Ricardo nodded and opened the door to the interview room. "I'll send him in a moment. You guys want coffee? Dad's gonna want some for sure."

"We'll take some if he's going to drink some," Michael replied. "Thank you."

"No worries. Hell, I'll pour myself a cup too. It's gonna be one of those days."

He left the three agents alone. Turk sat down and whined plaintively. Faith reached down and ruffled his fur. "It's okay, boy. We'll catch this son of a bitch."

"Or daughter as the case may be," Michael said. He shook his head. "You gotta have some level of rage to do this."

"Definitely," Faith agreed. "Like I said, this was personal. He wasn't just killing them; he was destroying them. He took the things they loved the most and used them to hurt Cassandra and Marissa in the most horrific way possible."

"I'm still liking romantic interest," Michael said. "That kind of hate grows from love more often than not." He grimaced. "Christ, did I actually say that out loud? Ugh. I need to get out of this job."

"Two and a half years until you earn your full pension," Faith reminded him. "Just endure until then."

"Why? You're not sticking around for yours."

Any further conversation on the subject was curtailed when the door opened and a stooped, elderly man shuffled into the room. Faith and Michael stood, and Turk instantly trotted to the man's side as Ricardo led him to the chair. He helped the old man sit, then nodded to the agents. "Fifteen minutes, okay guys? Funeral director's here."

"Understood," Faith replied.

Ricardo left the room, and Faith got her first good look at Mr. Holt. He was old, but not so old as he appeared to be at first glance. Faith figured he was in his late fifties or early sixties. The stooped shoulders and pallid face were due to grief, not weakness.

"I'm Samuel Holt," he said in a voice as tired as his body. "I guess you're the ones going to find out who killed Cassie?"

"Yes, sir," Faith said.

Sam nodded. His eyes were flat, not because he wasn't devastated but because he was still in shock. "They won't tell me how she died. They only say they believe it was homicide. That means she died bad."

It was a statement, not a question, and Faith decided not to pursue that line of thought. "How often did you speak to Cassie?"

"Every week," he said. The ghost of a smile crossed his lips. "She was my little girl. Even when she grew up and spread her wings, she was always close to me and her mother. She was a good girl." His smile faded. "Did they shoot her?"

"Who?" Michael asked.

"The people who killed her."

“Do you have reason to suspect more than one individual was involved?” Faith pressed.

Sam met her eyes. “You’re not going to tell me either, are you? How she died.”

“Probably not,” Faith admitted. “You can request full reports from the department if you want them. Right now, I want to focus on finding the individual or individuals responsible. You’ve twice suggested it might be more than one person. Can you tell me why you think that?”

“I have no idea,” Sam said. “I don’t even know if it was more than one. I just said people because… well, I don’t know.”

Faith tried another angle. “Did Cassie have a lot of friends?”

“Oh, not really, I guess. She had friends from school she talked to online, but no one particularly close. Everyone moved away. She was the only one who stayed close by.”

“Did any of those friends visit her?”

“I’m not sure. I imagine they saw each other around holidays when they came to visit their families, but I don’t know beyond that.”

“So you didn’t know her friends well.”

“Not since high school. Cassie was always a good girl. She hung with a good crowd, didn’t do drugs, didn’t get in fights, kept her grades up. All of her friends did the same thing, so Martha and I never had a reason to hover.”

“What about relationships? Any boyfriends or girlfriends give you cause for concern?”

Sam chuckled. “Cassie didn’t really have boyfriends. She would… well, enjoy herself, I guess is the polite way to put it. She was very popular with the boys.”

“Any of them seem the obsessive type?”

“Well, not in high school anyway. I didn’t know anyone else—none of them really stuck around long enough for me to know them—but I know Cassie would have told us if she was afraid of anyone. The only person who ever worried her was that one anti-war nut who camped out in front of her bakery last year.”

Faith’s ears pricked up at that. “Tell me about that.”

Sam shrugged. "Oh, you know how it is with kids. They get hooked on a cause, and it becomes their reason for existence. There was a guy from the University of Chicago who organized an anti-war protest in front of her business. Cassie was upset because the Veterans Day sale was going to do really well for her. She really does care about the troops, too. Her cousins all served, and even though they don't see each other a lot, she's proud of them."

"Were there ever any altercations between them?" Faith asked.

"Not physical ones. A couple of shouting matches, but nothing physical."

"Anyone get heated but the two of them?"

Sam chuckled. "No. The protest ended up being a non-starter. The guy picked a vegan bakery to pick on with a bunch of college students. Most of them ended up becoming customers. The one guy stuck to his guns, I'll give him that." He cocked his head. "Trent, I think his name was. Yeah, that's right."

"How was the situation resolved?"

"He showed up to protest on Veterans' Day, and the line was nearly a mile long. Cassie was offering free muffins to veterans. Guess Trent thought better about getting in the way of hundreds of combat veterans and their breakfasts."

"Did Trent have a last name?"

"He did, but I don't recall it. I honestly felt bad for his family."

"His family? Why?"

"It's a terrible thing burying a child." His shoulders slumped. "I know how that feels now."

Faith's heart sank. "Trent died?"

"Yes. Got hit by a drunk driver a week after the protest ended. Knocked off of his bike into a streetlamp. Gruesome way to go." He frowned. "Is that how Cassie died? Did she get hit by some asshole driving drunk?"

"No," Faith said, fighting to keep disappointment from her voice. "I can't tell you how, but I can tell you it wasn't a drunk driver."

Sam nodded, then sighed again. "My poor little girl." He looked at Faith and smiled softly. "She was about your age. Had the same blue eyes too." He shook his head. "The world's a terrible place when good people get killed for no reason."

"Yes," Faith agreed. "It can be."

They left Mr. Holt to his grief and headed to a nearby sandwich shop to eat and strategize. Turk happily devoured a cheesesteak over Michael's objections. "He's sleeping on *your* side of the room."

Michael ordered a cheesesteak himself—ironically—and Faith got a club sandwich. Michael made the mistake of calling it a hoagie and had to apologize profusely to the sandwich shop employee who gruffly informed him that it was "just a damned sub sandwich."

While they ate—on the patio to spare the offended employee from having to look at them—they discussed what they knew so far.

It wasn't much. Or rather, it was a considerable amount that was missing the crucially important parts.

"Marissa and Cassandra are both artisans," Faith said.

Michael shrugged. "I mean, I guess so. I love vegan muffins as much as the next guy, but I don't think baking is quite on the same artisanal plane as sculpting."

"It matters here, though, because our killer murdered them according to that art. The sculptor crushed by a sculpture; the baker poisoned by her bread.

"We also have the veterans connection. Marissa didn't care about veterans, but she was commissioned to build a piece for the Memorial Day celebration at the Museum of Modern Art. Cassandra *did* care about veterans, and she organized a very successful bake sale for them."

"So one person supports veterans in a professional way and the other in both a professional and personal way," Michael summarized. "Here's my gripe: Marissa was building some abstract art piece. Cassandra was tried-and-true red, white and blue. I get going after her if you hate the troops, but Marissa's just capitalizing on the whole schtick."

"In other words, profiting off of war."

"Yes, but that opens up a ton of potential victims. So why Marissa? Why her specifically? That's why I still think it's someone who knows both of them."

Faith sighed. "Yeah. I don't disagree with you, but where's the evidence? PD hasn't seen anything on social media indicating a connection. No names pop up in both women's lives. Marissa never bought from Cassandra's shop and Cassandra never visited MoMA. There's nothing there."

"Nothing we can see," Michael corrected. "Contrary to popular belief, not all of human existence plays out on social media. There's a chance that they had something going on that they didn't want to share with the world."

"There's also a chance that it was a one-off encounter that only matters to our killer," Faith added. She sighed and ran her hands through her hair. After a moment, she said, "We need to keep digging. If you're right, and there is a personal connection between these two, then we need to find it."

Michael looked at Turk. "Any ideas, big guy?"

Turk swallowed the last of his sub and looked plaintively back at the sandwich shop. Faith chuckled and ruffled his fur. "I'll buy you another sub, but it's going to be meatball this time. No more cheese for you."

Turk's reply indicated that he was perfectly fine with that.

After Turk finished his second sub, the three of them returned to the precinct. Ricardo set them up in a conference room and informed them that Dave's Donuts offered ten percent off to law enforcement should they feel themselves in need of refreshment.

The two FBI agents thanked him, but when he left the room, Michael spoke for both of them when he said, "Fingers crossed we won't have to be here that long."

Faith thought of Cassandra's face, the horror in her expression as she saw her own death come for her. "Yes," she agreed, "fingers crossed."

CHAPTER SEVEN

The killer watched from afar as the glassblower entertained a crowd of children by sculpting a figure of a soldier holding an assault rifle.

Was it called sculpting when it was glass? The killer wasn't sure. Blowing? Whatever. The point was that she was making an idol to warfare and doing it in front of children no less.

"Support our troops." How was it that after so many millions had died in pointless conflicts that didn't even take place on American soil thos,e three words still captivated society?

"Support our troops." Why? What were they doing to benefit humanity? What were they doing to benefit America? What were they doing to benefit themselves? Might as well say, "Support the colonization of Pluto." Even that would be better, because at least Pluto wasn't actively killing people.

The police, of course, were missing the damned point. "Local artist crushed to death by sculpture." "Local baker found dead in her own bakery." For Christ's sake, think about it! Ask *why*, damn it!

How about, "Whore who profits off of warmongering smothered by her own filth?" Why not, "Bitch who drives peaceful citizens away so murderers can get free food chokes on her own bile?" Why the hell was the world protecting these people?

A cheer distracted the killer from these thoughts. The glassblower had finished her figure and was now setting it to cool on a small display case. The kids grinned as though she'd just cured fucking cancer or something.

Well, that was okay. Tomorrow's headline would be, "Windbag who preaches genocide suffocates on her own hot air."

The glassblower looked the killer's way and smiled. The killer returned the smile and even a wave. *Rot in hell, you fucking bitch.*

The killer moved on. Tonight, the glassblower would close down her booth and pack everything into her trailer. She would drive to her home in Eastvale, and she would work on something else. That's all she did. Work, work, work. Blow, blow, blow. Celebrate murder, celebrate murder, oh God, I just love me a piece of murderer.

No more. The killer would make sure of that. The killer was under no illusions that killing these few would end all war or even any war. In the grand scheme of things, this might only be a drop in the ocean.

But it would be something. It would be one voice speaking out against sanctioned violence. The killer had to believe that would count for something.

If nothing else, it would put a smile on the killer's face.

Save your oxygen, brat. You'll need it.

CHAPTER EIGHT

Michael polished off the last of his donut and tossed the paper into the wastebasket. He pointed at Faith's half-eaten cruller. "You gonna eat that?"

"Be my guest," she said.

Michael took the cruller, wrapped it in another square of wax paper and squeezed hard. When he was satisfied he had pulped the donut as much as he could, he tossed it into the wastebasket too.

Faith understood his frustration. It was nearly eight o'clock in the evening. They had spent the past six hours looking into every aspect of Cassandra Holt's and Marissa Stone's lives from birth to present. There was nothing at all to indicate involvement with each other.

"We did our best," she told him. "We can't say we didn't."

"Then why?" He got up and started pacing. "There has to be a reason."

"Not always. David Berkowitz just shot random people out of his apartment. Henry Lee Lucas and Ottis Toole picked random people up off of the street. Sometimes there's no rhyme and no reason."

"Yeah, but there's never some rhyme and no reason. It's either random, or it's purposeful. There's no in-between. This guy is purposeful. I know he is. Or she. Or they."

"I agree," Faith said. "Our killer definitely isn't choosing randomly, but his reasons might not be anything we can understand. He could have picked them because they reminded him of girls in his high school art club who made fun of him. He could have picked them because he has something against pretty people. He could have picked them because the voices in his head told him to."

"That's David Berkowitz."

"Exactly."

"So what do we do? Do we stop looking for a reason and just start interrogating everyone in Chicago with access to pesticides?"

"Ricardo already followed up with Marten when we filled him in. He's going through Marten's customer list. So far, it's not looking promising."

"What about the chem lab where he gets his stuff?"

"That's in Indonesia, remember?"

"Right."

He sat down next to Faith with a heavy sigh. "I just know if we find that connection between them, we find our killer."

Faith leaned back and let her thoughts coalesce. "I'm still liking the veteran angle. You're liking the personal angle. What if it's both? What if there was a third person connected to them because of their support—genuine or otherwise—for veterans?"

"That would be a bonanza," Michael agreed, "but how do we find that third person?"

Faith thought a moment. "Let's call the local VA. They might know something."

Michael nodded. "Worth a shot. Who's going to answer this late, though?"

"Chicago's a big city. I'm willing to bet they have a night shift."

"Your mouth to God's ears."

Faith looked up the number and dialed while Michael made coffee. It was, as Ricardo had predicted, one of those days.

The person on the VA's end answered in a gruff and tired voice that Faith had heard far too often from veterans. "Chicago Veterans' Association. This is Art. What can I do for you?"

"This is Special Agent Faith Bold of the FBI. We're investigating the murders of Marissa Stone and Cassandra Holt. Can we ask you a few questions?"

"Me? Were they members of our VA or something?"

"No, sir. However, they both were involved in projects to support veterans, and we believe their killer might have targeted them because of that."

Art sighed. "Jesus. We fight and die for our country, then come home to fight and die because our country doesn't accept us. Makes you wonder why the hell we wore the uniform in the first place."

"I wore mine for the people who do accept us," Faith offered.

"Yeah. There seem to be less and less of them these days."

"Art, can you look up our victims and see if you can find anything in the VA's database that would link them either together or separately to initiatives to support veterans?"

"I can put a request in, but these things take time. Unless the project was recent, it'll get sent up to the national database, and they've got decades of data there."

"How soon is recent?"

“Three years.”

“That should be plenty. Thank you, Art.”

“Don’t mention it. Hey, you said you served?”

“Yes, sir. USMC. Two tours in Afghanistan, one in Iraq.”

"Ooh rah. I was a Marine, myself. Don't call me sir, though. Sir, you say for useless people."

She grinned. “First sergeant?”

"Hell, yes."

“Then thank you, First sergeant.”

Art hung up, and Michael said, “Is it true what they say? You can take the Marine out of the Corps, but you can never take the Corps out of the Marine?”

“You were with me in Washington. You tell me.”

In central Washington, Faith and Michael had investigated a murderer who targeted people he believed were warmongers. One of the victims was a Marine Corps Gunnery Sergeant whose platoon rallied in support of the two agents and helped catch the killer before he could murder another one of their own.

The parallels between that case and this one were unsettling. Once more, they were hunting someone who hated war, and once more, the VA could hold the key evidence they needed.

“Well, I’m beat,” Michael said. “I say we go to the hotel and catch come early shuteye. Odds are, they won’t find anything ton—”

Faith's phone rang before Michael could finish. She answered and put it on speaker. "Go ahead, Gunny."

“The sun must shine on you today, Marine. I got a result from a year back with both your girls’ names.”

Faith grinned. “What do you have for me?”

“Artists for Troops Experiencing Remorse. AFTER. Crappy name, but it was their idea.”

“Some sort of PTSD support, I’m guessing?”

"Exactly. They wanted to put together an art fair to raise money for veterans with PTSD. Most I had to do with it was tell them to try to pick a name that wasn't godawful." He chuckled. "They didn't take to that well. I remember the one girl, the artist. She told me if I wanted their help, I shouldn't be such a stuck-up priss about it. I explained to her calmly that PTSD wasn't the same thing as remorse, and if they wanted to help people, they needed to make sure they didn't alienate them."

"When you say calmly, do you mean Gunny sergeant calmly or civilian calmly."

Art laughed loudly at that, and Faith's spirits lifted slightly. The case might be stuck at the moment, but at least she had made a fellow veteran feel better. "Just as calmly as I'm speaking to you."

"Was anyone else involved with the project besides those two?"

"Sure was. Sylvia Waters. Eleanor Swift and Lila Voss."

"All women, huh?"

"Yeah, they wanted to showcase women in art making a difference. That was their angle. Anyway, I'll send you what we have. I hope you find whoever did this. That sculptor might have been rude, but no one deserves to be murdered."

"I'll do my best, Gunny. Thank you."

"What the hell did you just say? I didn't catch that."

This time, it was Faith's turn to laugh. "I said I absolutely will, Gunny sergeant."

"That's what I thought you said. Good luck, Marine."

"Thank you, Gunny."

He hung up, and as soon as Faith opened her email, she saw the VA file for Project AFTER.

"All right," Faith said. "Let's open this up."

The project contained a brief page with contact information for the two victims and the other three involved with the project. The next page was the proposal. Faith skimmed it and memorized key points.

The goal, as Art said, was to raise money for veterans with PTSD. Marissa would make an art installation depicting a child laying a flower on a gravestone topped with a combat helmet. Sylvia Waters, a glassblower, would make colored glass figurines of soldiers, sailors, pilots and military vehicles. Eleanor Swift was a painter. She would create a series of tribute paintings depicting veterans from all of the major wars, along with discounts for commissions on behalf of veterans and their families. Lila Voss was a potter and would make a ceramic mosaic mural of the six branches of the Armed Forces. Cassandra would bake veteran-themed muffins and cupcakes for the attendees.

"It doesn't look all that bad, except for the name," Michael said. "It's too bad it never got off the ground."

"It looks like it did get off the ground," Faith said as she continued to read. "They had a space reserved in Lincoln Park, seller's permits and they were talking to television and radio channels for advertising spots."

Michael lifted his eyebrows. “Damn. What happened?”

“Looks like things just stopped abruptly. No notice, they just stopped meeting.”

“Any way we can get the minutes of that meeting from your Gunny friend?”

She shook her head. “No, the meetings didn’t take place at the VA. This is all just the proposal. Whatever conversations were taking place between them took place elsewhere.”

“So how is it that there’s no evidence at all that Cassandra and Marissa knew each other? How do Cassandra’s parents not know her, or at least about her? Nothing in their social media about each other, the project or these other three women.”

"That last part actually makes sense. These kinds of projects are usually kept under wraps until things are set in stone. That way, if something falls through, it doesn't destroy the reputations of those involved."

“Makes sense,” Michael said. “You don’t want to hype up doing something for veterans and then not do it. Makes you look like an asshole.”

“Which is exactly what you don’t want if you’re also using this as a way to advance your reputation as an artist.” Faith rubbed her chin. “I’m thinking that they had a falling out. I think that’s why things stopped abruptly and why they didn’t ever have a public relationship. Something happened, and the project ended, and since these five women were connected via the project, their relationship was never recorded anywhere.”

Michael shook his head. “No, they had to have known each other somehow before this. How else would they think to start this project? They just meet drunkenly at some bar and decide to commit substantial time and money into an art fair?”

“Stranger things have happened. The idea for Southwest Airlines was written on a napkin and hashed out over a single dinner.”

“And then immediately formalized and recorded.”

“Yes, but these are artists, not businesspeople. Egos abound in both worlds, but operational sense only abounds in one.”

“Good point. Still, I can’t imagine that there isn’t something out there that will shed some light on this.”

“There is. Three things, in fact.”

Michael caught her point. “So we should call a few numbers and see what kind of information we can get.”

"We'll start with Sylvia Waters. She lives closest to the precinct. It's late, but not too late, especially for an artist. We might get lucky and catch her before she goes to sleep."

"Or heads out to murder one of the other two."

The door to the conference room opened, and Ricardo poked his head in. "Guys? You might want to come with me on this one. It's a doozy."

Faith and Michael shared a sober look. "Another body?" Faith asked.

"Yes. Looks like the same guy."

Faith's heart sank. "Dare I ask the name of the victim?"

"Woman named Sylvia Waters. She's a glassblower who lives in Glenview."

Michael shared another look with Faith, this one grim.

Once more, they were too late.

CHAPTER NINE

"I'll give our guy this," Michael said. "He's creative." When Faith didn't reply, he asked, "Too on the nose?"

"Just a bit," she said drily.

Sylvia Waters stared at the two agents from inside of a nine-foot diameter glass globe. More glass formed an eagle that sat perched on the globe. The anchor was unfinished, but the banner above the eagle that read SEMPER FIDELIS left no doubt that this was meant to be the Marine Corps logo.

"Her husband is deployed," Ricardo informed them. "Germany. Slated to come home next month. I guess this was supposed to be a surprise for him."

Faith looked at Sylvia's body, which lay pressed against the interior of the globe, face purple and eyes bulging with asphyxiation. "Surprise."

Turk was sniffing around the studio—a converted guest home on the property with the second floor completely removed to allow more space. At the moment, the globe and the tools used to create it were the only things in the studio. The rest of her work had been moved to the home's garage.

"Well, we know for sure that it's related to the project these women worked on," Michael said. "That's a plus."

"Ricardo," Faith said. "I need the police department to get a hold of two women ASAP. Just before you walked in, we discovered an abandoned art fair project that all three of our victims collaborated on. The other two women are either suspects or potential victims."

"Names, addresses and horn digits, and I'll get right on it."

"Off topic," Michael said, "but I absolutely love the term horn digits, and I'm using it instead of phone number from now on."

"Gotta find whatever joy you can when you work a job like ours," Ricardo said without a hint of humor.

Faith gave him the contact information for Eleanor Swift and Lila Voss. "I'll get started on this," he told the agents. "You guys get what you need, then tell Marco to send CSI." He looked at Sylvia's body. "Jesus. Our guy's a sicko."

"You don't think it's one of these two women?" Faith asked.

"Unless one of these two women wrestles professionally for a living, I doubt they're forcing her into her own glass bowl and then keeping her there while they close the glass."

He had a point. Sylvia was a sturdy six-foot-one and one hundred sixty pounds. At the same height and forty pounds bigger, Michael might have been able to take her in a fight, but he and the similarly sized Marco were the only people present who would have had a good shot. Still, they could have been working together, and if they weren't perpetrators, they were almost certainly targets.

"See if they'll accept protective custody. That's something you can offer, right?"

"Considering that three of their friends have been killed in five days? Yeah, I think we can swing it."

"Good."

He left, and Faith and Michael walked around the room. Nothing appeared to be disturbed at first glance, but it was hard to tell with the studio almost empty, and what was there was left sort of lying around rather than organized in any way.

"The rod's gone," Michael said.

"The what?"

"The rod. Glassblowers use a rod to shape the molten glass as they're working it. It's not here, so our killer must have taken it."

"He didn't wear gloves last time," Faith said. "I'm betting he didn't wear any this time and realized that he left prints on the rod."

"Yeah well," Michael said, bending over and picking up a piece of torn black plastic, "it looks like he remembered to cover his shoes. Garbage bag. The heavy-duty kind like they use for yards."

Faith pulled out a baggie, and Michael deposited the evidence. "Keep looking. He's being careful but not too careful. I think we could find something here."

"Hope springs eternal."

Faith stood and looked at the back of the globe. The killer's addition to the piece was obvious. While most of the work flowed seamlessly and showed no obvious deformation, a five-foot by four-foot chunk of the back was warped and bumpy and coarse-textured. The killer had sealed the hole, but he hadn't made it look pretty.

Not that it really mattered.

Except… "He incapacitated her first," Faith said. "We need to get to Sylvia's body. He rendered her unconscious before putting her in here. There's no way he gets her in here without this piece being ruined. He put her inside, sealed it, then waited for it to cool so he knew she wouldn't be able to break through it."

"Would he really have waited for it to cool?" Michael asked. "It's not like she's going to run through molten glass."

"If it's that or die, she would. She would have come out with serious burns, but she would have had a chance of surviving."

Michael grimaced. "I think I'd rather die than survive that."

"That's easy to say until you're actually faced with death."

"Fair enough, but I stand by what I said."

"Well, if anyone wants to bury you behind molten glass, I'll make sure to pass that information along."

He frowned at her. "Hey, that was uncalled for."

"Look around for a glass cutter," Faith said. "I want to get prints off of the body before we turn it to CSI. We might be able to get answers sooner that way."

Michael looked around the haphazard piles of tools before finding the glass cutter. He picked it up and asked, "May I do the honors? I've always wanted to be a jewel thief."

Faith rolled her eyes. "Go ahead."

Michael pressed the suction cup to the globe while Faith and Turk watched from a safe distance back. Faith half-expected Michael to do something clumsy and bring the whole thing shattering down on them, but he deftly applied the cutting oil and opened a four-foot-wide hole in the globe. He grunted with effort as he lifted the glass off of the globe and set it carefully down next to the sculpture.

"Whew. I forgot how heavy glass was."

"You did that way too well," Faith said. "When you die, are we going to find the cash from the Federal Reserve Robbery last year stashed somewhere on your property."

"Of course not. I would never be foolish enough to hide it on my property."

Faith chuckled, but her humor vanished when Michael pulled Sylvia's body out of the globe. She looked almost as bad as Cassandra did, which made sense since both women died essentially from asphyxiation, Cassandra's chemical and Sylvia's mechanical.

Turk bared his teeth and growled low in his throat. "You smell something, boy?" Faith asked.

Turk walked to the body and sniffed. When he reached Sylvia's throat, he barked, then moved off. Faith followed him, calling back to Michael, "Check her throat for ligature marks and fingerprints."

Turk walked in a circular path to the back of the globe and from there around until he reached the front door. He put his nose to the latch and barked again, then headed down the yard. Faith paused long enough to verify the scratches that indicated the same kind of forced entry as at the previous two crime scenes, then followed Turk.

Turk walked ahead a few yards, then veered right. Faith followed him to a patch of trees behind the house. He stopped at a clearing and barked once more, then stilled.

Faith noticed two strips of flattened vegetation and followed them with her flashlight up the hill into the woods beyond. The ground was too thickly carpeted to leave tire tread marks, but Faith knew that their killer had to have a four-wheel-drive vehicle with offroad tires. There was no other way he would have made it down this far without running into trees and getting stuck.

This would be what? The seventh or eighth killer with a truck? The Big Three truck companies should start advertising that capability. Buy our new half-ton, it's a great getaway vehicle for psychopaths.

"Good boy, Turk."

She called Ricardo and told him about the truck.

"Damn. Good job, Turk. We just assumed he came in from the front. I guess now we know why the neighbors didn't see him. Doesn't explain Marissa's apartment building, but it does show that he's being thorough. Not that that's good news. I'll send a vehicular crimes team out to look at the tracks. It might look like there's nothing helpful there, but they can find things us normies wouldn't know to look for. One time they found a guy because they found a drop of differential fluid that matched a specific model year Suzuki."

"Here's hoping they can pull off another miracle. Speaking of miracles, any luck getting a hold of our girls?"

"No answer to the phone calls. We're sending officers to the addresses right now."

"Good. Keep me posted."

"Will do."

She rejoined Michael inside. "So our guy's got a four-wheel-drive truck or SUV. Turk found tire tracks in the hill to the east."

"Damn. What is it with killers and trucks?"

"I mean, if anyone needs to get places other people can't go."

Michael nodded. "I guess when you put it that way."

"So what about Sylvia?" Faith asked. "Any prints?"

"Prints, no. Ligature marks, yes. Bad ones. She was strangled with a thin cord. Could have killed her that way if he held on a few more seconds, but he didn't."

"How can you tell?"

"They welted up badly. If she had died, the welts would be smaller or not there at all." He grinned at her. "Look at me remembering my college criminology courses."

Faith gave him a thumbs-up. "The gruesome things that please us." She looked at Sylvia's body. "And I use the word please very loosely."

"So we have two things confirmed," Michael said. "These five women are the targets, and he's hellbent on killing them in a way that relates to their own art. Even when he could kill them other ways, he wants them to die like this. This is the first time he's actually shown himself to the victim, though."

"That confirms a third thing," Faith said, "he's not a coward. He didn't hide from Marissa and leave Cassandra's scene because he was afraid, he just adjusted his MO to match how he wanted each victim to die."

"So how is he going to kill a painter and a potter?"

"Potter burns in her own kiln," Michael said. "No clue with the painter."

Faith grimaced. "Yeah, I forgot that potters have ovens."

"Has Ricardo gotten a hold of them yet?"

"No. No answer to the phones. He has officers on their way to the addresses now."

"Good. I think you and I are done here unless you can think of something else."

Faith shook her head. "Have Marco send for CSI. Sorry about the no sleep, but I'm moving that we go back to the precinct and start digging into Sylvia Waters to see if we can find someone else who might be our killer. There's no way that all five of these women successfully purged all memory of their interaction together."

"I like your optimism," Michael said. "Maybe one day I'll share it."

They headed down the drive to the street and told the waiting Marco that the scene was his. Then the three agents headed back to the precinct.

Turk usually spent drives sitting in between the two human agents and waiting patiently until they reached their destination. This time, he stood on all fours, eyes focused straight ahead and tail switching back and forth.

He could smell their killer now. He was on his trail. Faith smiled slightly and scratched him behind his ear. "Good dog. Let's get this bastard."

CHAPTER TEN

"Veronica Chase."

Faith looked up at Michael and lifted an eyebrow. "Do tell."

Michael grinned. "Don't mind if I do."

He sat next to Faith and turned his laptop so she could see his screen. An image of a burly woman in her late thirties appeared on the screen. The woman was smiling, but her eyes were hard, and her smile looked a lot more like a wolf baring its teeth than an expression of happiness.

"Miss Chase is also a glassblower. For six years straight, she won Best Large Piece in *Pipe and Rod* magazine."

Faith smiled drily. "Wonderful name."

"Only if you have a dirty mind. More pertinently, she was hailed as the greatest glassblowing artist in the United States up until five years ago when a certain Miss Sylvia Waters burst onto the scene with an intricate sculpture of a child meeting Santa Claus that debuted at the World's Fair. Since then, Sylvia's won Best Large Piece every year running. This year would have been year number six."

"With the eagle, globe and anchor piece."

"Exactly. That would have tied Chase's record and, according to this editor, erased all doubt that Miss Waters is the greatest fine artist in their profession. Miss Chase, the one-time darling of the glass art world, was unavailable for comment, but her social media page makes her opinion clear enough."

Michael clicked to another tab and showed an image of Chase's social media account next to a post that read, *Lovely to see that* Pipe and Rod *has jumped on the bandwagon of cheap, mindless pop art filth that does nothing to advance society or make a point other than to show how some young glassblowers can manipulate trends to serve their chintzy, watered-down version of art."*

"She sounds very gracious and mature," Faith said.

"That's what I thought. As an aside, she's also six-foot-three and two hundred fifty pounds."

"More than big enough to handle Sylvia."

"Exactly."

Faith checked the time. It was nearly midnight. Chase would almost certainly be in bed.

That was too bad. Ricardo hadn't found Elizabeth and Lila at their homes, but Elizabeth's roommate told him that she was due back from her convention tomorrow morning, and Lila's social media suggested she was known to pop in and out of her home at odd times.

Meaning that at any moment, their lives could be in danger. Veronica Chase would have to wake up and convince the two agents that she had nothing to do with these murders.

"I'll pour us some coffee for the road," Michael said. "She's about a forty-minute drive away, so I'll need to stay awake."

"I can drive," Faith offered.

"And I can skate, but you don't see me offering to pull you along on a board."

"No way you can skate."

"Exactly."

She rolled her eyes and followed Michael to his car.

***

Veronica Chase lived in Naperville, which, as Michael predicted, was a forty-minute drive West of the city. Her house was a spacious three-story Victorian that sat on four acres of well-manicured lawn interrupted by flower gardens and well-pruned trees dominated by a central fountain made of ornately blown and colored glass. Victoria Chase might have an attitude, but Faith had to admit that when it came to artistry, she did seem to occupy a higher plane than Sylvia.

Imagine how much it must frustrate her to watch Sylvia steal her spotlight.

Surprisingly, Victoria Chase was still up when they knocked. She answered the door with a frown. "It's almost one o'clock in the morning. What the hell are you doing here?"

Michael pointed at the bright white logos on their uniforms. "Guess."

Victoria's scowl deepened. "I paid my taxes, if that's what you're getting at."

"It's not. We're here to talk about Sylvia Waters."

Shock crossed Victoria's face, temporarily dispelling the scowl. "What? Why are you talking to me about her?"

"She was found dead in her home about two hours ago. Someone entombed her alive in her own creation."

"Huh. Well, that sucks. But I had nothing to do with it."

"You mind if we ask you a few questions?" Faith asked.

"Yes. Piss off."

She made to close the door, but when Turk growled, she hesitated and took a step back. She looked up at Faith's and Michael's stony faces and said softly. "Oh God. You think it was me."

"We don't think it was anyone yet," Faith said, "but you look pretty good right about now."

"Oh God. Oh…" she caught herself and said, "Look, it's late. Can I come to the station sometime tomorrow and talk?"

Faith looked at Turk. The dog growled, baring his teeth in a smile not unlike the one Chase wore in her picture. Victoria paled and made to close the door again. As she was closing it, Faith called. "You drive a truck, Miss Chase? Four-wheel-drive?"

She paused with the door half-closed and said, "I have a Ford Super Duty. Why?"

"Because that's probable cause," Faith informed her, "and now you don't have a choice but to talk to us."

Veronica sighed. "Son of a… All right, come in. Don't expect me to offer you coffee or anything."

"Fine with us," Michael said. "We already had our coffee."

"Good for you."

The three of them stepped inside. Veronica looked uneasily at Turk. "Does the dog have to come with?"

"Yes."

Turk growled at her, and she sighed. "All right. I guess I don't really have a say in the matter."

"You really don't."

She rolled her eyes and led them into a spacious living room. The coffee table was also of glass, and when Veronica noticed them looking at it, she said, "That's one of mine too. I went through a thing in my twenties where I wanted to make everything I owned out of glass. Some bullshit 'living in a glass house' phase. I actually wanted to make a glass house, but even for a rich girl, that's a prohibitive amount of money. Not that it matters, anyway. My time in the sun has set."

"You don't think you're poised to take over the spotlight now that Sylvia Waters is out of the way?" Faith asked.

Veronica scoffed. “Hell no. I’m poised to spend the rest of my career having my name printed next to ‘if only Sylvia was alive. Just imagine how incredible *she* would have been.’ If you guys are looking for a motive for me to kill her, trust me, there isn’t one.”

“Not to be an asshole,” Michael said, “but it kind of looks like things were kaput for you no matter what happened to Sylvia. So I’m thinking the motive is, ‘you took everything from me, now I’m going to take everything from you.’”

“Cute.”

“Not really.”

Veronica sighed. “Look, I don’t know what to tell you. The answer’s no. I didn’t do anything to her. Why would I do that? I might be pissed that she stole the spotlight from me with her pop culture pandering bullshit, but I still have money. I can drown my sorrows with champagne from Champagne. I can go buy a sports car or three if I want to cry about it. I know I’m bragging, but whatever. I can still enjoy life. A lot more than I would enjoy it in a nine by six cell.”

“No doubt,” Faith agreed. “But sometimes people get angry. Sometimes wealth isn’t enough. Sometimes people don’t think about the things they’re going to miss until it’s too late.”

Veronica glowered at the agent and said nothing.

“Let’s start with how you knew Sylvia,” Michael said.

“Everyone in glassblowing knew her. She was the Steph Curry of our art. You can’t be in glass art and not know someone who won a major award five years running.”

“But you knew her personally.”

“Are you asking or guessing?”

“Doesn’t matter,” Faith interjected. “You’re going to tell us, or we’re going to be very unhappy.”

Veronica chuckled. "You're already unhappy. And I'm not going to make it easier for you to convict me of a crime I didn't commit. Yes, I knew her personally. We met at the convention, where she beat me for Best Large Piece the first time. She did a statue of Little Bo Peep. Can you believe that? Little Bo fucking Peep beat out a thirty-foot panorama of a Pennsylvania Dutch town made out of a single piece of glass. I had detailed villagers inside that town. I put in the details of the beards the men had. And she beat me with a cartoon sheep that looked like a storybook cloud with a potato for a head."

“That must have been frustrating,” Faith replied.

"Frustrating? It was goddamned embarrassing. You know why they were doing it too, don't you? Just because Miss Sylvia Waters looks like every man's dream. Sure, she's a little tall, but she's got the body shape and a winning smile. Meanwhile, I look like an old farm girl who might have walked right out of that village. When there were no pretty girls in glassblowing, the art mattered. Soon as the Hourglass Figure starts shaking her hips, suddenly everyone wants a piece."

It appeared that Veronica was jealous of more than Sylvia's success as an artist. "Did you ever confront her about her art?"

"No. I invited her several times to talk to me, but she never did. I called her out in magazines and online, but all that bought me was the chance to be called a sore loser."

"You don't think you're a sore loser?"

She lifted her hands and let them drop. "Hell, I don't know. I guess so. But can you blame me? For God's sake, how is it that Little Goddamned Bo Peep beats…" she sighed, and her anger faded away. "Look, this is all I had."

"What about the rich life?" Michael reminded her. "You know, the trio of sports cars and stuff?"

"I'm not saying I'd rather go to prison than lose this," Veronica snapped. "But… I mattered. You understand? I mattered. I was worth something. Now?" She lifted her hands and let them drop again. "Now I'm worth nothing again. Now I'm just the has-been." She shook her head. "I spent three hundred hours on that glassblowing piece. Two months of my time meticulously shaping every single piece of it until it was perfect. I paid attention to the posture of the old man driving his dairy cart to market, the look on the child's face as she watched a mother bird feeding her chicks, the slope of a young bride's shoulder as she nervously awaited her husband at the altar. That was *life!* That was *real!* And I get upstaged by some bimbo with perky tits who did a children's book character."

She looked at Faith. "When do you need an alibi? I have security here. I can give you one. Wait, you said two hours ago, right?"

"She was discovered two hours ago. I need one for the whole night."

"I can give you that."

She picked up her remote and switched on the TV screen. "If you need me to send you a copy of the file, I can do that too, but here you go. Watch and enjoy."

She clicked the remote a few times until she pulled up security footage from that evening. Faith watched as she rewound from that moment. When she saw the image of the three of them walking in reverse from the house to their rental car, she sighed. She allowed Veronica to keep going back until her own car reversed out of the garage at six-thirty pm. Then she said, "All right. That's good enough. Thank you for your time, Miss Chase. For what it's worth, I think you're an outstanding artist."

"I appreciate that," Veronica replied. "But we both know that's not worth shit. To either of us."

Faith looked back at the security footage to see Veronica leaving her vehicle and walking into her house, taking Faith's case with her.

"Count your blessings, Miss Chase," she said. "You got to come home tonight."

Veronica held a defiant expression for a moment before her gaze faltered. She lowered her eyes and kept them there as the three agents left her house.

CHAPTER ELEVEN

Faith jogged down her street, heading south toward the park. Turk kept pace at her side, trotting easily and sniffing the air ahead of them. The morning was unusually foggy, but the glow of the streetlamps provided Faith enough light to see the sidewalk ahead.

This early in the morning, there was little noise. An hour from now, the neighborhood would wake up, and Faith's return journey would be accompanied by the soft rumble of car engines and the occasional snippet of conversation from those who chose to walk or avail themselves of public transportation. But for now, the only sound was Turk's softly padding footfalls and Faith's own somewhat louder steps.

They reached the cross street where Faith would turn to the park, and Turk trotted ahead a few yards, eager to put his feet into soft, damp grass rather than hard, cold concrete. Faith smiled ahead at her dog and felt the same rush of love she always did when she and Turk ran.

She looked ahead for the park, but the fog thickened considerably out of nowhere, and all she could see was the next few yards of sidewalk. She frowned and wondered if the weather was changing. This kind of pea soup fog only occurred if the day was going to be unseasonably warm or if a powerful nor'easter was blowing down from Maine. She really hoped it was the former.

A soft echo came to the back of her mind, an impression more than a sound. The echoes followed her own footsteps, but they didn't sound like echoes. They sounded more like...

She stopped suddenly. The echoes continued for three more footfalls.

She was being followed.

She whirled around, but all she could see was the damned fog. "Hello?" she called back. "Excuse me?"

No answer.

"If you're following me, that's a really bad idea. I'm a trained FBI agent, and I guarantee you I've taken down more dangerous people than you. Go back and tell the guy you're working for to come after me himself if he wants me so badly."

No answer.

Faith huffed and turned around.

Turk was gone.

The unease in her mind immediately turned to fear. "Turk? Hold up, boy."

She started forward again, jogging, then running, then sprinting. "Turk? Turk! Where are you?"

Her dog didn't answer.

This wasn't right. Turk would never leave her. Not like this. Not when someone was following her. He would lay down his own life before he allowed any harm to come to her. Someone must have taken him.

"Turk! Asshole, if you hurt my dog, the wrath of God will seem like a kiss from your grandmother when I find you!"

No answer but the echoes, which grew louder and louder.

Her fear slithered from her brain to her spinal cord, overwhelming her thoughts and forcing her into a dead run straight ahead. Thoughts of Turk faded as the primal fear of death overcame everything. Somewhere in the back of her mind, she knew this wasn't real, but her mind held no power here. She was prey, and a predator was chasing her.

The echoes grew louder and louder until they weren't echoes anymore but the thick, heavy footfalls of something not quite human. Sour breath wafted toward her, and her nostrils flared. A shadow loomed over her, and she opened her mouth and—

***

She sat up, gasping. Turk was immediately at her side, licking her face. She grabbed him and hugged him fiercely, her fear still gripping her and refusing to cede place to her mind. Turk barked in alarm and wrestled free of her, barking and growling as he circled her, looking for the creature that dared to frighten his partner.

Michael got out of bed instantly, moving faster than Faith had seen him move in years. He brought his gun up and switched on the light. When he saw Faith, a look of irritation flashed across his face, fast enough that he probably didn't even realize it before that look switched to one of compassion.

That look finally snapped Faith out of her funk. She sighed and lowered her eyes, rubbing her forehead with her fingertips.

"Faith? It's okay. No one's here."

"I know," she said. "Yeah, I'm sorry. It was just another nightmare."

"Trammell?"

"Yeah. I think so. I don't know. It was different this time."

"What was it?"

Faith concentrated, but the details faded. All she could remember was crying out for Turk in the middle of a sea of fog.

"Forget it," she said. "It's just the case. I'm just pissed that we can't find the killer."

"Well, we'll get him. Don't worry." He checked his clock and added, "It's five to six, anyway. We needed to be up." He grinned at her. "At least you didn't sleep in this time."

She glared and stuck her finger up at him, and he laughed. "Hey, since you're up, you want to go get breakfast for us?"

"Hey, since you're up, you want to kiss my ass?"

"See? You're over it already. Nothing to be afraid of."

She rolled her eyes and said, "Just for that, I'm bringing you decaf."

"You wouldn't dare."

"Watch me."

She left the room, Turk glued to her side. He watched her carefully as she headed to the elevator, and when it opened, he jumped ahead of her and sniffed around thoroughly before finally barking to let her know it was safe.

She smiled at him as she stepped inside. "Good dog."

He dipped his head professionally and focused on the door. She chuckled and ruffled his fur. "Easy, boy. Let's not frighten the other guests."

By the time she returned to the room—with caffeinated coffee after a bit of soul-searching convinced her she didn't want to deal with an uncaffeinated Michael—she had put the last of her anxiety behind her. Michael was on the phone and held up a finger for Faith to be quiet. Faith set the food down and listened in as he talked.

"Yes, sir. I appreciate it. Yes, my partner will be here. I'll put you on speaker now."

He set the phone down and pressed the speaker button. "Go ahead, Mr. Ambassador."

Faith's ears perked up. She looked at Michael and mouthed, *Stone?*

Michael nodded just before the ambassador said, "I understand you're pursuing leads in my daughter's murder."

“Yes, sir,” Faith replied. “We believe it might be related to a project your daughter undertook with the other two victims and two other women.”

“Two victims? I thought there was only one more.”

Damn it. “The second victim is very recent. I shouldn’t have even brought it up.”

“Don’t worry, I’m not going to rat you out. I *am*, however, disturbed that this individual is still out there and possibly killing more women as we speak.”

“I assure you, sir, we are doing everything in our power to—”

“Relax, I’m not here to throw a fit, either. I’m here because I have a lead.”

Faith’s ears perked up again. Michael ran to grab a pen and notepad and Faith said, “What’s that lead, sir?”

“My wife and I were checking our daughter’s phone records—we paid for her plan—and we came across a disturbing series of texts between Marissa and a man she had saved only as ‘Asshole.’”

“At the risk of jumping to conclusions, the name sounds appropriate.”

“It is. This guy was the worst brand of liberal nutjob. Called all soldiers murderers and called Marissa a collaborator for agreeing to take on the MoMA Memorial Day job.”

“Did he say anything threatening?”

“Not directly, but he repeatedly told her that she deserved to die.”

“That’s close enough. Did Marissa respond to him at all?”

Ambassador Stone sighed. “Typical young and stupid arrogance. Called him an idiot and an asshole and told him that she wasn’t even doing anything soldier-related. She was doing real art, and if he had a problem with it, it was probably… well, she wasn’t polite. I don’t think she took him seriously.”

“Did you see anything to indicate how she knew this person?”

“I guess they met at an art convention. There are a few texts from a couple months ago that seem innocent enough. He wanted her to meet him for lunch to give him some advice on his sculpting career. She turned him down, and he took it well, said he wasn’t trying to look for a date, but he understood if she wanted to keep her distance. Said he admired her work, and if she ever changed her mind, he would love to have the perspective of a ‘real sculptor.’”

“When did the tone of the texts change?”

"The week before she died. He sent her a text saying he heard that she was working on a project for the Memorial Day celebration and how he couldn't believe that she was actually supporting the murder of babies and pregnant women. Things actually managed to go downhill from there."

"Did she ever tell you about this guy?"

Stone scoffed. "No. Marissa was very independent. She didn't like us being involved in her life, and… well, she wasn't always the most intelligent when it came to people. She was an artist through and through. The world was her playground, and people were just there. She didn't hate them, and she didn't love them. She sure didn't understand them. You should have seen some of the boyfriends she picked. That last one would be lucky to hold down a job at a burger joint."

"She didn't seem any different to you? Anxious or paranoid? Like someone was following her?"

Michael frowned questioningly at Faith, and Stone said, "No, she didn't. But that doesn't mean anything. Someone could have put a gun to her head, and she wouldn't have understood she was in danger. She just…" his voice softened and took on the same exhausted tone that colored Samuel Holt's voice in his interview. "She just didn't understand things. We tried to teach her, my wife and I, but I was a congressman and then a Senator and then an Ambassador and… she…"

"I'm sure you did your best, sir," Faith replied. "Listen, I need the number for Asshole. We're going to find him, and if he's as much an asshole as he seems to be, we're going to make him answer for what he did to your daughter."

"Thank you," Stone said. "Give me your number, and I'll send the video."

Faith read her number to him and when she finished, she said, "I may call later with more questions, Mr. Ambassador. I understand that your schedule's busy, but if you can get back to me as soon as possible, that will really help me as I try to find justice for your daughter."

"I'll answer as soon as I can. Good luck, Special Agent. Thank you. I'm sure you don't hear that enough."

She smiled. "I hear it plenty, sir, but it's always appreciated."

When he hung up, Faith turned to Michael. "You ready for the number?"

"Got the Driver License Database primed and ready."

She read him the number, and seconds after he typed it in, a name popped up.

Garth Holbrook looked exactly like the Asshole he seemed to be. He had a glare that made his weak chin and soft eyes look weaker and softer, but his info stated he was six-foot-eight and three hundred pounds.

"We'll want backup for this one," Michael said. "I'm too old to fight football players."

"Agreed," Faith said. "I'll call Ricardo."

"I hate to jinx it," Michael said, "but do you think he might be our guy?"

"We need to establish a connection with him and the other victims," Faith said, "but I have a good feeling about this one."

"That's good enough for me."

CHAPTER TWELVE

The killer had to hand it to these women. They were indefatigable.

That was a good word, indefatigable. It meant essentially the same thing as relentless or driven, but details mattered. Indefatigable meant "persisting tirelessly." Relentless meant persisting without stopping, but indefatigable meant persisting without even losing energy. An unstoppable force of nature.

Unfortunately, that's what the U.S. military was: a force of nature that consumed and destroyed without regard to the people who suffered from its actions. All that mattered was what they wanted and needed.

And their supporters were just as indefatigable. Maybe it was something about the scent of blood that drove away all of their ability to think and forced them to act as though the only purpose of their existence was to maim and kill. Some metal band had probably written a song about that.

Not that the killer listened to metal.

The particular indefatigable woman the killer watched now wasn't even being paid for her work. She was just doing it.

"It" was a mural which depicted an army of Americans boarding naval vessels to go fight some war overseas. A title banner at the bottom center of the mural announced it as "Freedom's March."

That was rich. The killer actually laughed out loud at that. Thankfully, the car window was up.

The light turned green, and the killer proceeded smoothly ahead without looking back at the abomination behind. Freedom's March. Freedom to do what? To kill people across an ocean who aren't fighting you and don't give a damn what you or anyone else in the United States does? To waste billions of taxpayer dollars every year so the government can build better bombs and stealthier airplanes to drop them instead of researching cures to cancer and Alzheimer's disease and kidney failure?

Freedom's March.

The killer wished there was a way to make the painter march to her death. That would be fitting. But some things were out of reach, so the killer would have to make do with the resources available.

That would be all right. It all fit the theme.

The killer was growing famous. The news had finally realized that the Artisan Killer (stupid name, but whatever) wasn't just going to limit himself to a victim or two. No, the killer had a mission, one that they still didn't quite understand but one that would drive the killer to take more victims, as many as needed to complete the mission.

It occurred to the killer that he needed to think about what came after these women were dealt with. There would have to be a plan for the next one and the one after that.

In that one way, the killer supposed, these women shared something in common with the killer. Once you start, you can't stop. You become relentless, driven.

Indefatigable.

The killer smiled and accelerated smoothly onto the freeway as he continued the journey home.

CHAPTER THIRTEEN

Faith, Michael, Turk and four police officers quietly approached Garth Holbrook's house. Four more police officers waited on the street with long guns pointed at the small ranch home.

"Nice and quick, boys," Ricardo said softly. "I want a minimum of fuss."

Michael knocked on the door and stepped back. Faith heard shuffling as Garth approached the door. He looked through the window, and his eyes widened when he saw the officers surrounding his house. He opened the door a crack and said in an incongruously soft and high-pitched voice that reminded Faith uncomfortably of Jethro Trammell's, "Hello? Can I help you?"

"Garth Holbrook?" Michael asked.

"That's me. Is everything okay?"

"No, sir, everything is not okay. We need to ask you some questions. Can you come out here and talk to us?"

"Um… what's this about?"

"Marissa Stone, Cassandra Holt, and Sylvia Waters."

Garth's eyes widened again the moment Michael mentioned Marissa. "Oh, shit," he said glumly.

"Oh shit," Michael agreed.

Garth slumped. He looked docile, but Faith had seen docile giants flip in a heartbeat. She kept her hand on her weapon and maintained a safe distance as Garth stepped outside.

"Do I have to go to jail?" he asked.

"We'll figure that out," Michael said.

"Well, do you think maybe I should? I mean… I don't really want the neighbors to hear everything."

Faith and Michael exchanged a look, then looked at Ricardo.

"We can do that," Ricardo said. "You'll have to wear two pairs of handcuffs and go in the back of one of our cars, and you'll have to convince me that I don't have to worry about you doing anything stupid, but if you can do that, I'm fine taking you somewhere you won't be embarrassed."

Garth nodded. "Yeah, that's fine. I know I fucked up. I just don't want people staring at me."

Ricardo nodded to the two biggest officers he had. They were still dwarfed by Garth, but the big suspect remained calm and allowed himself to be handcuffed and led to a vehicle.

As they followed Ricardo back to the station, Michael asked Faith, "What do you think? The whole gentle giant thing an act?"

"Might be," she said, "might not be. I've seen people his size flip before."

"Hell of a flip to go from meekly following a police detective into his vehicle to crushing someone with a statue."

"Most serial killers don't present themselves as serial killers. Many of them manage to be well-respected members of their communities right up until the bodies are found in their backyards."

"You're telling me. Remember that guy from Philly who buried people alive for being bad neighbors."

Faith smiled slightly. "Horace Greenwood. Yeah, I remember him. I fingered his son for the Copycat Killer."

"Oh yeah, I remember that now. The Boss nearly fired you for breaking into his house and going full cowboy on him. Turned out he was just a drug dealer, right?"

"Yeah. Hated his dad. Blamed him for his mother's death."

"Didn't Horace turn out to have actually killed his wife?"

"I can't remember. Wouldn't surprise me. That guy had the affect of a sheet of paper."

Michael shook his head. "It really sucks, you know? The least these assholes could do is look like assholes."

"Some of them do. Kenneth Langeveldt was a certified creep no matter who you talked to."

Kenneth Langeveldt was currently serving consecutive life terms for paralyzing people to serve as stand-ins for the family he had burnt to death as a teenager. He would use a cocktail of animal tranquilizers and stimulants to paralyze them, then keep them alive until they dehydrated or their hearts gave out. The three of them had chased him into the woods behind his house and captured him after a prolonged struggle which nearly saw him kill Faith.

"See, I liked him," Michael said. "There was no wondering with him. You looked at him, and right away you knew, 'Yep, he's a psycho.' Then again, he got away with it for years before we caught him, so maybe other people didn't see what we saw."

"People don't want to see evil," Faith observed. "They'd rather believe that most people are decent, or at least indifferent. No one wants to look around at their friends and neighbors and wonder which one of them likes to butcher people alive. So they blind themselves to it."

"Yeah. Can't go wrong with a classic. Put your hands over your eyes and say, 'La la la, you can't see me.'"

An image flashed through Faith's mind of running through thick fog while heavy footsteps gradually approached. "If only it was that easy."

***

When they reached the precinct, they stopped to talk with Ricardo before interviewing Garth.

"How was he?" Faith asked.

"Meek as a lamb," Ricardo replied. "Kept his head down. Didn't talk much, but when he did, he was polite and softspoken. Creeped the hell out of me to be honest."

"You think he's the guy?" Michael asked.

"I don't know, but he's creepy either way. The guy looks like he could crush a handful of walnuts as easily as you or I pop a soda can, and he talks like he's afraid to raise his own voice."

"If I could crush a handful of walnuts with my bare hands, I'd be afraid of losing my temper too," Michael opined.

"Especially if the walnuts I crushed were three women," Faith added.

Ricardo shivered. "Well, for the first time in my twenty-three years as a detective, I'm glad he's not my problem. Good luck, agents."

The three of them walked into the interrogation room and took their seats opposite Garth. Faith noticed that Turk kept his feet and watched the big suspect warily.

Garth noticed it, too. He smiled sadly and said, "Yeah, I scare a lot of dogs. I don't mean to, but I'm a big guy. I think I look like a bear to them or something."

"You'd look like a bear to some bears," Michael said.

Garth chuckled. "Yeah, I know. My mom always said I must have had giant blood in me."

Faith brought the conversation back to the point. "Do you know why you're here, Mr. Holbrook?"

He slumped a little. “Yeah, I know. I said some nasty things to Marissa online, and now she’s dead, and it looks like I did it.”

“Did you?”

“No. I was angry at her, but I didn’t kill her. I wouldn’t do that to anyone. I know I’m big, but I’m not mean.”

“You said some things that were pretty mean.”

He slumped further. “Yeah, I know.”

"You said that she deserved to die. That all people like her deserved to die and that the world would be a better place without them in it."

He lowered his head and didn’t respond.”

“Why were you so angry with her?”

“She was working with the Memorial Day project. I just…” he frowned. “Why are we celebrating killers? I don’t get it. Why not have a Memorial Day where we celebrate and honor the innocent victims who were killed? Why do we talk about soldiers who died in Japan and not the factory workers incinerated by nuclear weapons or the laborers melted by incendiary bombs? We talk about Holocaust victims and the horrors that other nations inflicted on people, but we don't talk about the villages we massacred in Vietnam or the cities we blew to rubble in Iraq. It's hypocritical."

His face slowly grew angrier as he spoke, and his voice rose in pitch. He caught himself after a moment and paled a little before reddening. Faith prodded a little more.

“Do you believe that people who celebrate Memorial Day deserve to die?”

“No, I just… Really, why do we celebrate war? We say we’re a peaceful society, but then we have two whole holidays dedicated to war. We don’t have any holidays dedicated to victims. None that anyone celebrate anyway. When’s the last time you heard about Holocaust Remembrance Day or Pearl Harbor Day?”

“I read a piece about Pearl Harbor Day last winter,” Michael said.

Garth scoffed. “Yeah, where? Some online blog.”

Michael lifted an eyebrow. “If I say yes, are you going to fly into a rage?”

“No, but…” he tried to lift his hands, but the shackles prevented him. “That’s my point. You can’t get away from Honor our Nation’s Trained Killers Days.” He shook his head. “It just makes me angry.”

“Why Marissa specifically, though?” Faith pressed. “Why single her out?”

"Because I used to admire her. She was the best sculptor in the world. I'm a sculptor too. If you'd come inside, I could have shown you some of the things that I make. But I'm like the guy who sits on the street corner playing guitar for dollar bills. She's like Eddie van Halen or Jimmy Page. It's crazy just how she thinks of those things."

His face changed again, becoming bright with excitement and admiration. He shifted emotions very easily. Faith could see now how he could have experienced an overpowering moment of rage.

But could he had held onto that rage long enough to sneak into Marissa's apartment, hide behind a statue and crush her with it?

"So it hurt more when you felt that she was supporting killers."

"Of course it did. It was terrible. I didn't know what to do except be really mad."

"Mad enough to kill her?"

He realized his mistake and paled again. "No. Just… I wanted to scare her."

"Why?"

"Because she deserved to be scared!" Garth shouted. "Because she was…" he caught himself and lowered his voice. "Look, I get it. You're going to tell me she wasn't doing anything for veterans. She was just using that as a springboard to promote her own art. She created a random statue of some guy thinking, and it just happened to be going to a Memorial Day exhibit. That's what she told me, but here's the thing: why not just say no? Why not deny them the right to use your work? Plenty of people do it. They take a stand. She not only wouldn't take a stand, but she laughed at the idea that she would have to take a stand. Like I was stupid for feeling the way I do."

"So you took it personally."

"Yeah, I did. And so should you." His eyes narrowed slightly. "Except you probably do support the troops, don't you? You probably agree with everything they stand for."

Faith considered revealing her service in the Marine Corps to see how he would react, but she had already determined that he had poor emotional control. If she pushed him too far, he would completely lose himself, and then they wouldn't be able to get information from him.

"I don't believe any innocent person should be murdered," she replied. "I believe Marissa Stone was murdered. My job is to find out who murdered her and make sure they can't murder anyone else."

"And you think that's me."

"I'm sure you can understand why," Michael said.

Garth sighed. "Yeah. Yeah, I know. Like I said, I know I fucked up." He lifted his eyes to them and said pleadingly, "but I didn't fuck up that badly. Okay? I didn't kill her."

"Are you happy that she's dead?"

"No, I…" He sighed once more and dropped his head to his chest. "Look, you guys think it was me already. I don't have an alibi. I was home alone, but there are no cameras or anything, so I can't prove it. I just need to talk to a lawyer and hope they can convince you."

"I'm not convinced that you did it yet," Faith said.

"You *sound* like you are."

"I'm trying to figure it out. You say you have no alibi, which is bad. You said she deserved to die, which is worse. You clearly get very angry at anyone who even comes close to supporting troops, which fits the profile our killer showed in all three murders. That's probably the worst."

He frowned. "Wait. All three murders?"

"Yes. Marissa Stone, Cassandra Holt and Sylvia Waters."

Garth leaned forward, suddenly excited. "When were the other two killed?"

Faith and Michael shared a look. "Cassandra was killed two days after Marissa was killed, and Sylvia Waters was killed last night."

Garth sighed with relief. "Then I *can* prove it wasn't me. I was home last night, but Marissa died… Five days ago?"

"Correct."

"Okay, so that makes Cassandra Holt's death three nights ago. Yeah, that was Thursday night. I was in Milwaukee Thursday night. I spent the night at the Lakes Hotel. I was there because the Bucks were playing the Lakers. I missed the Bulls-Lakers game because I was sick, so seeing the Bucks play them was the last chance to see the Lakers." He blushed a little. "I grew up in LA, so I'm a Lakers fan. I try to see them whenever they're in town. The game didn't finish until after midnight, so I stayed the night in Milwaukee. I think you can check security footage at the arena to show that I was at the game, and then you can check the hotel to show I wasn't even in Chicago when Cassandra Holt died."

He sighed with relief and said, "Okay. I feel better now."

Faith could understand that sentiment, but she didn't feel much better herself. She looked at Michael and saw the same disappointment in his eyes. "We'll follow up on that alibi, Mr. Holbrook.

Ten minutes later, Faith and Michael stared glumly at security footage from the Lakes Hotel and Fiserv Forum. The massive Garth Holbrook might have been upper average for a basketball player, but he was a hulking and unmistakable giant among the fans, and it was even clearer at the hotel.

They were back to square one.

The agents managed to do a passable job of keeping professional demeanors as they delivered the news to Garth. Garth managed to do a passable job of being respectful of the fact that the loved ones of three innocent women would once more be denied closure.

As Ricardo unshackled him, he made eye contact with Faith. "I'm not glad that she's dead," he assured her. "I was mad, but I didn't want her to die. I don't think anyone should die. That's why I hate war so much."

Faith nodded. "Well, do yourself a favor and don't tell people online that you wish they would die. You were one basketball game away from three life sentences."

He returned her nod with a vigorous one of his own. "I won't. I learned my lesson there, that's for sure."

Ricardo led him away, leaving two very frustrated Special Agents and a somewhat relieved K9 behind. Turk looked up at Faith, and when he saw that she wasn't as relieved as he was that the massive threat was gone, he cocked his head curiously.

"Well," Michael said. "Another wasted morning. Really makes you want to dance for joy."

Ricardo came back. The stoop in his shoulders and the dejected look on his face told Faith that the news was only going to get worse.

It did.

"Guys. We have another body."

CHAPTER FOURTEEN

Eleanor Swift was the youngest of the victims and looked it. At twenty-eight, she was only a year younger than Marissa Stone, but she had a cherubic face and youthful figure that made her look like a college student.

At least, she would have if she hadn't been bloated and coated to unrecognizability with scarlet acrylic paint.

"How did they find her?" Michael asked.

"They didn't. They called the police because they heard screaming. The responding officers came, and the door to the house was ajar. They checked the house thoroughly and didn't find anyone. They filed the missing persons report, and the dispatch officer recognized the name and sent it to my office. I was the one who suggested they look through anything related to painting. Can't say I expected this, though."

The fifty-five-gallon drum of blue acrylic paint now held about thirty gallons. Ten or fifteen had spilled onto the floor in the process of removing Eleanor's body. Another gallon coated her thickly from head to toe. The rest of the paint was inside her and was now leaking out through all of her orifices.

Faith once more felt her stomach turn. The paint fumes mixed with the image of the bloated and dead woman forced her to turn away and step outside. Turk followed her for a moment before Faith waved him back inside and said, "Go investigate, Turk. I'll be okay."

She stepped into the fresh air and breathed deeply. The moon looked like a chunky, misshapen egg, the shape described for reasons Faith couldn't remember as gibbous. As a child, she had loved the egg-shaped moon and pretended that it was the massive belly of the man in the moon. Now, it looked pallid and lifeless.

She turned away from the moon and exhaled another deep breath.

It was odd that this affected her so much. She'd seen horrifying crime scenes before. She'd seen people cut to pieces and exsanguinated. She'd seen people's muscles and tendons cut so that they looked unrecognizable as human. Less than a week ago, she'd seen the aftermath of a woman around Eleanor's age crushed by a three-quarter-ton statue.

But something about Eleanor Swift disturbed her more than any other. Maybe it was the sight of the paint leaking from her nose and eyes. It evoked an image of being consumed by something from the inside out.

"You okay?"

Faith turned to Michael, who stood a few feet from her, his face lined with compassion. "No," she admitted. "No, I'm not. This woman was being drowned in her own paint while we were busy interrogating a guy who turned out to be another dead end."

"Do we have to have the 'you can't blame yourself' conversation?" Michael asked.

"No, but…" she lifted her hands and let them drop. "It just sucks. I know it's nothing we haven't seen before, but… I keep thinking of Eleanor drowning and struggling, pounding on the lid and hoping desperately that someone, anyone might hear her and rescue her. Then no one does."

"We have the worst job in the world in a lot of ways," Michael said.

"Yeah. Damned straight. I had an easier time surviving combat in the Marine Corps than I'm having catching murderers for the FBI. Maybe that's part of why I'm so upset. What does it say about me that I had an easier time—"

"Nothing," Michael interrupted sternly. "Not a damned thing. Garth seems like a decent guy at heart, but he's an idiot, Faith. He has no idea how the world really works. He has no idea that for all the decent, peaceful people alive, there are people who want to hurt, kill and steal from those decent people, sometimes for no other reason than because they can. If we don't have people willing to do what they need to do to protect the decent people, then we leave them to the mercy of the murderers."

"Not all of the people we fought were killers," Faith replied. "A lot of them were people who were just doing what we were: protecting the decent people in their own lives from people who wanted to hurt them."

"I'm not a psychologist," Michael said. "So I can't tell you what to do about those feelings. I *can* tell you that you're not a murderer. I can also tell you that war is shitty and innocent people die along with guilty people. That was something Garth got right. But it doesn't make you a bad person for fighting for your innocent people."

She sighed and turned back to the garage where Eleanor Swift's body was just now being loaded onto the coroner's gurney. "Yeah. You're right. Let's go fight for that innocent person."

They walked back up to the large backyard patio that served as Eleanor Swift's outdoor studio. In addition to the drum of blue, other drums held red, white, pink, purple, brown, black, white and green. Smaller drums held more exotic colors, and three of the larger drums held primer.

"She was working on a mural," Ricardo said. "In Lincoln Park. Supposed to honor soldiers from all of the major wars of the twentieth and twenty-first centuries. That's why there's so much paint."

"I thought we were trying to get a hold of her," Faith said. "What happened to that?"

"She didn't answer our phone calls. We sent people to her house, and she wasn't there. We left messages saying that she was in danger and needed to call us, but she kept ignoring them."

"You couldn't send officers here to watch her place?"

Ricardo shook his head. "The department doesn't offer bodyguard services, and no one had made explicit threats to her. The chief didn't consider the evidence we provided as damning enough to send officers to watch the home of a private citizen without their approval."

"So I can assume that no one is watching Lila Voss's place right now."

"I'll try again," Ricardo said. "He might be willing to listen now. But frankly, Lila's going to have to start answering her phone too. Personal freedom's a bitch sometimes, but I'm not going to convince the city to do away with it."

Faith sighed irritably. "Why the hell would she refuse protection? Did she think you guys were spammers?"

"I don't know," Ricardo said with equal irritability. "Maybe you should ask her."

"Maybe both of you should control your emotions and do your jobs," Michael scolded. "The Police Department tried to protect her. Their help was refused. It sucks that she died. It's not any of our fault. We've all been working our asses off to stop this guy. We didn't get to it in time. Let's act like law enforcement and bury the emotions until we get home and drown them in alcohol."

Ricardo chuckled bitterly. "Don't push me, agent, I'm a half-step from that already." He sighed and said, "Well, the good news is that our killer left us some more to work with. We have an ID on the vehicle from one of the neighbors. Midsize truck with oversized off-road tires and a turbocharged engine. A neighbor heard the engine screaming a few minutes after hearing the woman scream and got a glimpse of it.

Bright metallic blue. That's an easily recognizable color. I'm putting the APB out now."

"Do that," Faith agreed, "and see if you can get any fingerprints or footprints. If she was able to scream before she was subdued, then our killer had to rush this. He's bound to have made some more mistakes."

"We'll do that," Ricardo promised.

He left to issue instructions to his men, and Faith joined Michael. "Call the Chicago Field Office," she said. "I want agents outside of Lila Voss's house ASAP. I don't give a shit how she feels about it. I want to talk to her too. Maybe hearing it from a couple of irate FBI agents will convince her that she really is in danger and she'll stop acting like a goddamned moron."

"The sun should rise in a few hours. We'll probably be wrapped up here by then. Or, we'll get lucky, find a fingerprint and a suspect and catch the bastard before he gets a chance at Voss."

"Fingers crossed."

They examined the scene and tried to put together a sequence of events. A palette with much more reasonable amounts of acrylic paint sat on a small table with three brushes coated in different colors of paint. The table and a folding chair sat in front of an easel with a half-finished canvas self-portrait.

The portrait was technically masterful, if not particularly innovative. It was a typical head and bust of a young woman—Eleanor herself. She was posed so that her arm covered her breasts, but her heavy-lidded expression, lips slightly parted, indicated a great deal of sensuality.

"Self-absorbed," Faith commented.

"What artist isn't?"

"Good point."

"Besides, Cassandra Holt wasn't self-absorbed. She gave out free cupcakes to veterans."

"I don't know. You could argue that was just a marketing tactic and that she expected to make more money from it in the long run."

"Do you think that being self-absorbed is one of the reasons our killer is taking these artists?"

"Maybe. It might explain why these women specifically and not other people who support the troops."

"But does that help us find him? It's got to be someone who could access all of them. We're still looking for a personal connection."

"I know. I'm just trying to put myself in the killer's mindset. He doesn't like war. Hates soldiers. Hates people who support them. He sees these five women—all attractive—and sees that they've achieved success in their chosen art form. He probably doesn't have natural talent or he does but he never acted on it, and he resents them for this success. Then he sees that they're using their talent to make money off of supporting veterans. They don't really care about the veterans, they just want the money."

"So he flies off the deep end and starts killing them because they hit the trifecta. They're attractive and out of reach for him, so he lusts after them futilely. They're talented, and other people revere them for that talent, so it's a constant reminder that he's never going to have that talent. They're leveraging a cause he despises and don't even have the decency to support that cause. They're just using their talent for money."

"We need someone who interacts with them via art. Someone who lives around their betters every day but will never reach that level of success. Someone who could reasonably be expected to snap after prolonged exposure to these five."

"But who would be exposed to all of them?" Michael asked. "They were in each other's spheres for a few weeks, then fell out hard."

"A supplier or dealer or curator," Faith replied. "Someone who would interact with artists across all disciplines."

"Including bakers?"

"That could be the one-off. Maybe he came there for muffins."

"So we look at lists of people who dealt with these artists and compare them to transaction lists from Cassandra's bakery. Anyone who matches gets to be a suspect."

"Ooh, goody."

"All right. Well, we have a direction to go in now. Let's get the hell out of here."

The three of them left the scene, eager to escape the cloying scent of paint and death. On the way back to the station, Faith thought of their most recent victim. Young and arrogant enough to believe that death would never come for her. Foolish enough to think that whatever had prompted the killer to take her erstwhile associates wouldn't inspire him to come after her. Perhaps self-centered enough to think that no one could possibly want to hurt a creature as beautiful as she.

Or maybe, like most people, she just couldn't accept the violence in the world. So, she covered her eyes and shouted, "La la la, you can't see me."

Until someone could see her.

CHAPTER FIFTEEN

Faith sipped her coffee and took a bite out of one of Dave's famous donuts. She was warming up to them, but whether that was because she was actually growing to appreciate the greasy, cloying sweetness of the treats or because she was too exhausted to think clearly, she didn't know.

Cassandra's bakery was far more successful than Faith would have predicted. She had something in the neighborhood of two thousand customers over the past year, and many of them were regulars who returned at least once a week.

The list of people who interacted with all five of the artists was shorter, but still more extensive than Faith would have guessed. There were over a hundred individuals ranging from staff and owners at art galleries, curators at museums, editors and reporters for art magazines, dealers of various different supplies, agents, managers and the entourages associated with all of them. Since each employer represented had different databases and proprietary software, there was no swift way to cross-reference all of them. They had to do it manually.

"Christ, this is insane," Michael groused. "You sure we don't want the police department to deal with this?"

"I want them focused on the physical evidence. We might get a faster answer from that than from these lists. Did you call the Chicago Field Office?"

"Yeah, I called them. They have two agents watching the house right now, but they said she's not there."

"What about workplace?"

"She's an artist. Her home is her workplace."

"Are you sure or are you assuming." He glared at her, and she lifted her hand. "All right. Just asking."

"God, I'm exhausted," he griped, rubbing his eyes. "I really can't do these all-nighters anymore."

"Two and a half more years," Faith reminded him.

"Yeah, I know."

"How's Ellie feel about that?" she asked. "I know you mentioned she was trying to push you to leave earlier."

“She feels like I’m being an idiot. But she’s not fighting with me over it anymore. I think she gets that it makes more financial sense that way, but she doesn’t like that I’m putting myself in danger.”

"Well, hey, you haven't gotten hurt yet. Maybe if you come home without bruises, she'll be even more relaxed."

“Yeah. Hey, maybe if I workout a little bit, I can start for the Sixers next year.”

Faith rolled her eyes. “Okay, grumpy, be that way.”

The door opened, and a smiling Ricardo entered. “Good morning, my precious pretties. Guess what I have for you today?”

“A promise to never call us your precious pretties again?” Michael asked.

“Nope. A name. A good one. One who was a regular visitor to all of the victims so far and who was kind enough to leave a substantial amount of fingerprints in the home of one Eleanor Swift.”

Faith’s ears perked up. That would make this suspect the first one they could reliably connect to each of the victims since Gregory Marten with Marissa Stone and Cassandra Holt. “Who is it?”

“The wonderfully named Jasper Flynn.”

With a flourish, Ricardo produced an image of a good-looking man with dark curly hair and brooding features. "Mr. Flynn is a delivery driver for Art Supplies International. Don't let the mundane name fool you. They are the largest supplier of equipment, supplies, and media for artists of all sorts. And our three professional artists were on his route."

“Really? They live all over the city. How did they swing that?”

“How did *Mr. Flynn* swing that? I’m not sure, but his route looks like Mayor Thornberg’s idea of a voting district. Oh, and by the way, ASI allowed him to use his personal vehicle for his deliveries. Guess what his personal vehicle was?”

“A bright blue midsize truck with off-road tires?”

“The brightest and the bluest. Nice and garish and adorned with the latest technology in I-like-driving-really-slowly-over-big-rocks.”

“And the connection to Cassandra Holt?”

“Stopped there for a muffin and a coffee every morning. Would show up early to see her before he started his route. Methinks the boy liked the girl.”

“Wonderful,” Michael said. “I like this guy.”

“So do I. Too bad the girls never returned his affection.”

“Well, I’m sure he’ll find someone to hold him when he gets where he’s going,” Faith said. “Assuming he *is* our guy.”

Ricardo grinned. “Only one way to find out.”

***

Jasper Flynn was in the middle of a delivery when the police vehicle pulled up. When he saw Faith looking at him, his eyes widened. He ran for his truck, but Michael gunned the motor and pulled the car in front of the blue Chevy. Ricardo blocked the rear, and Jasper hesitated a second, then started to run.

“Turk! Go get him!”

Turk leapt from Faith’s arms and sprinted after Jasper. He latched onto Jasper’s leg, and Jasper released a scream that truly impressed Faith for its volume and extremely high pitch.

He shook Turk off of him, but by that time, the two human agents and two police officers had caught up to him. He might think himself tough enough to fight off a dog, but fortunately, he was wise enough to decline a contest with four automatic handguns.

“Don’t shoot!” he squealed in almost the same tone with which he screamed. “I surrender!”

“On the ground!” Ricardo shouted. “Give me your hands!”

He quickly cuffed Jasper and yanked him to his feet. “Nice truck, asshole.”

The officers placed the protesting Jasper into their car and read him his rights. Faith and Turk took a moment to examine the vehicle.

The truck definitely looked capable of navigating the rough terrain behind Sylvia Waters’ house. Scratches and dents on the underside proved that Jasper used it off-road. Turk sniffed carefully but didn’t notice any smell that stood out to him.

Then again, Jasper’s truck was pristine, newly washed. There might not be anything left for Turk to smell.

Ricardo approached and said, “We’ll have him nice and wrapped up for you at the precinct. You want the truck, or do you want us to impound it?”

“You can impound it,” Faith said, “but take a thorough look at the interior first. Turk didn’t smell anything, but there might still be prints or something inside that can help us.”

“We will do everything short of tearing it apart for scrap,” Ricardo promised. He looked back at the car. “Or maybe I will tear it apart for scrap. Just because.”

“Let’s wait until we make sure that it’s not evidence,” Michael offered.

The three agents were in good spirits as they headed back to the police station. Jasper had more of a connection to the victims than anyone so far, and his prints were all over Eleanor’s crime scene. They hadn’t confirmed that it matched the partial from Marissa Stone’s scene, but the truck fit the description given by Eleanor’s neighbor. When the police looked at the truck, they would be able to confirm it was the one used at Sylvia Waters’ house.

This felt good. This felt like a good chance at being their guy.

Jasper, not surprisingly, was more concerned about his truck than anything else when they reached the station. The moment Faith, Michael and Turk walked into the interrogation room, he asked, “What’s going to happen to my truck?”

“That depends,” Michael replied. “Are you a murderer?”

“What? Yo, screw—”

Turk growled, and Jasper’s momentary lapse into aggression vanished.

Now Faith knew that he was capable of aggression.

“Mr. Flynn,” she began. “We’ll get right to it. You are a person of interest in the murders of Marissa Stone, Cassandra Holt, Sylvia Waters and Eleanor Swift.”

“What? But I… oh, come on, man.” He leaned back in the chair, his face shining with sweat. “Come on, man, I didn’t do it.”

“No one did,” Michael said. “Lot of innocent people in prison.”

“I know, but come on, man.”

“We’re on, man,” Faith assured him. “Time for you to come on. Believe me, guilty or innocent, honesty is your friend. I start finding out that you lied to me, I start getting unhappy. You don’t want me to be unhappy, trust me.”

“Look, I just delivered them stuff, okay?”

“We’ll start there. How long did you know the victims?”

“I didn’t know them!”

“Really? You saw them at least once a month for the past four years. You saw Cassandra Holt five days a week in that timeframe.”

“She was off Thursdays.”

“Oh, my mistake,” Faith said with exaggerated embarrassment. “How silly of me. Only four days a week. I mean, that’s almost as much as I see my partner, but there’s no way you knew her, right?”

“I liked her muffins,” Jasper said.

“I’ll bet you did,” Michael replied. “Nice and sweet and soft. What else did you like?”

Jasper glared at him. “I get where you’re going with this, but we weren’t fucking, okay? She didn’t—”

He stopped himself just a little too late, and Faith prodded. “She didn’t what?”

Jasper sighed. “Look, she was pretty, okay? I asked her out, and she said no. End of story.”

"Really? Sure, you didn't ask her out again and again. Maybe enough that she got uncomfortable and told you to stop, or she'd kick you out of the store?"

“No! She… I mean, she told me to stop, but not like she was going to kick me out. She was just annoyed. I left it at that, I swear.”

“So we’ve gone from asking her out once to asking her out until she got annoyed by it.”

Jasper rolled his eyes.

“No, I like this,” Michael said. “We’re working our way to the truth. We’re going to figure all of this out together. This is a good thing. Come on, Jasper, buddy, lighten up.”

“Let’s move on to the others. Eleanor Swift. Your fingerprints were found… how did Detective Ricardo put it?”

“I believe he said, ‘all over her house.’” Michael said helpfully.

“Yeah. Something like that. Also, someone said they saw your nice little truck screaming tires away from her house a few minutes after they heard a woman scream.”

Jasper reddened. “They said that? That they heard a woman scream?”

“Yep. Woman screams, a few minutes later, a blue truck with absurdly large tires peels out from in front of her house. Almost like the driver was trying to escape a crime scene.”

“They’re not absurdly large. They’re thirty-fives. They’re the stock tires that come on the truck.”

“Oh, my mistake,” Faith said. “I’m so glad you corrected me. That’s the really important part: whether or not your tires make sense.”

Jasper sighed and began to tap his feet restlessly. Turk growled at him, and he stopped.

“I’m still waiting for an explanation,” Faith reminded him.

He groaned and said, “I was sleeping with her, okay? That’s why you found the fingerprints. I would make sure to deliver to her last because if she was in the mood, I could usually get her to let me bang her. She was one of those girls who was real open, you know? It's hard to find a girl like that."

"Probably hard to let a girl like that go," Michael said. "Might make a man mad if he does well by a girl for a while, and she decides she doesn't want it anymore."

"That's not what happened, okay? She still wanted it. We saw each other every week."

"So she was your girlfriend?" Faith asked.

"No, man, it wasn't like that. We just liked fooling around."

"Got it. So she's your friend with benefits."

"Not really a friend. We just hooked up. Come on, I'm a single guy. You know how it is."

"Can't say I've ever been a guy," Faith corrected. "So why did they hear her scream moments before your truck squealed its tires out of there?"

Jasper reddened. "They didn't hear her scream. They heard me scream."

Faith and Michael exchanged a look. "They heard *you* scream."

"Yeah."

Faith recalled the shriek he had released when they arrested him. Unfortunately, it was very believable that he could have released a scream like that.

"Say I believe you," she said. "What could have prompted that scream?"

He shivered. "I found her hand."

"Her hand?"

"She… it was sticking out of the paint bucket. I saw it, and I freaked out because I knew she must be in there. I called her name, and she didn't answer. So I touched her hand, and she… she was stiff and cold." He shivered again. "I freaked out."

"Why didn't you call the authorities?" Michael asked.

"I was scared! I was in her house, and I left my footprints and fingerprints everywhere. And I touched her hand. I was afraid they'd think I did it. And they did. You do. You think I fucking killed her."

Faith *had* thought he killed her. Now, she wasn't so sure.

She sighed and asked her least favorite question. "Can you confirm your whereabouts for six nights ago?"

"Six nights ago? I was at a club with another girl. We stayed until the club closed, then we…" he reddened. "Well, we went out to the forest, and I parked, and we…" he shrugged. "You know."

“Yeah, I think I do. Did this other girl have a name?”

"Come on," he said. "Do I really need to, like, involve her?"

“It’s either that, or we start liking you for four murders.” When Jasper continued to stare blankly at Faith, she sighed. “Yes. You need to involve her. Name and phone number.”

“I didn’t get her number. She was just a girl at the club. She told me her name was Candy, but that’s probably not her real name.”

Faith sighed. “What about the club?”

“Cityscape. It’s on Kingsbury Street.”

“Got it. Hang tight, okay?”

She and Michael stood to leave, and Jasper flinched. “Wait, you’re not going to take your dog?”

“Don’t worry,” Faith said on her way out. “He’s nice. Most of the time.”

Turk bared his teeth in a grin, and Jasper moaned.

When they were outside of the room, Faith asked, “What do you think?”

Michael shook his head. “It’s a little suspect. He was at a club, then with a girl who didn’t give him a name. He had a regular thing with Eleanor, but he was hitting on Cassandra enough that she had to tell him to back off. He delivered to all five women on a gerrymandered route—we haven’t even asked him about that yet—but despite the fact that we have witnesses placing him at the scene of a murder, potentially evidence placing him at the scene of another murder and established connections to all four of our victims we’re supposed to believe that he’s innocent? I don’t buy it.”

Faith nodded. “Yeah, me either.”

Her lips pursed, and Michael sighed. “But?”

“But I also kind of do. He’s a jumpy, insecure coward.”

“Our killer could be a coward. I know he got up close and personal a couple of times, but that’s clearly not his style.”

“He could be a coward,” she agreed, “but not jumpy or insecure. These murders took forethought and careful planning.”

“He could be putting on an act.”

“Maybe. Let’s get Ricardo to follow up with Cityscape, and we’ll keep going with Jasper.”

“I’ll go let him know. He likes women. Maybe he’ll open up to you more if I’m not there to threaten his manhood.”

She gave him a dry look, and he lifted his hands. “What? I’m a guy. I know how we think.”

"Think isn't the word I would have chosen."

"Well, we think with the little—"

"Got it," she interrupted. "I don't think I'm Jasper's type, especially after I had Turk hold him hostage, but I'll go see if I can sweat a little more out of him."

Jasper was staring in terror at Turk when Faith returned. He jumped when the door closed, and Faith said, "Relax. No one's going to hurt you."

"Going to prison for the rest of my life hurts."

"Well…" she took a seat and folded her hands on the table in front of him. "We're going to table the discussion about you and Eleanor for the moment. Personally, I find it strange that you would be sleeping with one girl regularly and picking up random girls from the bar while also obsessing over another woman enough that you showed up every morning at her muffin shop and asked her out enough to bother her, but I'm told that sometimes men don't think clearly when it comes to that stuff."

"I like her muffins."

"They're all right. They're not worth harassing a woman over."

"I already told you! She asked me to back off, and I did!"

"Wonderful. Here's my next question: How did you manage to get a route that stretches for thirty-six miles and looks like a snake?"

"What?"

"I've had it with the stupid act, Jasper. Answer the damned question."

"Okay, I…" he sighed. "Look, I like girls man. I like girl artists because they're easy." Seeing the expression on Faith's face, he added, "Yeah, I know. I'm a piece of shit. Whatever."

"So you arranged your route to make sure that everyone on it was a female."

"Yeah. The company doesn't care as long as you're on time." He grinned at Faith. "I'm always on time."

She returned a stony look, and his smile faded. "Next question. Where do you park when you make deliveries?"

His brow furrowed. "Park? In front of their houses usually."

"Never in the woods behind the houses?"

"No. I don't creep on them."

"So the police aren't going to match your truck to the tracks we found behind Sylvia Waters' house."

"No! I go off road, but not behind people's houses. I don't need to creep on people. I get girls the normal way."

"Not all girls."

"Enough girls."

"Does it bother you when girls reject you?"

"No, because another girl won't. There's a lot of you out there. More than one for each of us. I don't need to be pissed when one girl says no because I can go to a club, flash a smile and find a honey." He smiled. "Not every woman's like you. Some people think I'm hot."

The door opened, and Michael's face told Faith everything she needed to know. He looked at Jasper and said, "The girl's name was Shawna. She wants to know why you haven't called her back. If I were you, I'd call her back and thank her for being honest, because she just saved you a prison sentence."

"Hell, I'll call her back for—" Faith glared at him, and he swallowed. "I'll call her back."

Faith watched as Ricardo escorted the newly freed Jasper to the front of the precinct. With the specter of imprisonment lifted, Jasper was loudly protesting that if anything was wrong with his truck, he would sue the police department.

Michael shook his head. "Who the hell is this guy? How does he manage to get away with four murders and leave nothing behind we can use?"

Faith shook her head. "We'll find him. He has given us something we can use. We just need to figure out what it is."

"How many more girls die in the meantime?"

Faith didn't have an answer for that.

CHAPTER SIXTEEN

Eleanor Swift's sister held up somewhat better than Cassandra Holt's parents. Her eyes were red and puffy when Faith and Michael sat down to interview her, but her shoulders were straight, and her head erect.

It was two hours after Jasper Flynn had been released. Amanda Swift had identified her sister and after talking with the coroner, she had agreed to talk to the investigators. Faith could only hope that Eleanor looked a little better than she had when Faith saw her. No one should have that be their last memory of their loved one.

"Thank you for speaking with us, Miss…"

"Amanda," she replied, shaking Faith's and Michael's hands. "Thank you for talking to me."

"I'm sorry for your sister," Faith said, "and I'm sorry you had to see her like that."

Amanda shrugged. "They cleaned her up all right. She's not going to win any more beauty pageants, but she doesn't look like a horror show either."

She lifted a napkin to her eyes, and Faith saw her hands shaking. She put on a brave front, but inside, she really wasn't holding up any better than Samuel Holt. She put the napkin down and looked at Faith. "Have you found him yet?"

"Not yet. We're pursuing some leads, but we haven't found a suspect yet who hasn't had an alibi."

She sighed. "Figures. Eleanor was a… free spirit, shall we say? Didn't think to be cautious about who she kept company with. If he was hot, he was in bed with her." She smiled tightly. "Sorry. Not the most wonderful thing to say about my sister, I guess, but it's the truth. I figured one of them would end up getting her one day."

"So you believe it was a paramour of hers?"

Amanda laughed bitterly. "Paramour. That's a nice word. So proper. And to answer your question, if it wasn't one of her fuckbuddies, who would it be?"

Faith folded her hands on the table. "We believe that your sister was a victim of a serial killer. We don't believe her death was isolated."

Amanda's eyes widened. "A *serial* killer? Who?"

"The same killer who murdered Marissa Stone, Cassandra Holt, and Sylvia Waters."

"I don't know any of those people. Should I?"

"Their names have been in the news for the past week. Not all at once, but that's how long since the first killing."

"See, I don't watch the news. I just get tired of all the doom and gloom. Of course, it would happen that the doom and gloom strikes right at home." Tears came to her eyes, and she shook her head. "A serial killer. God."

"We believe this killer is targeting artists," Faith said. "Specifically, artists involved in an art fair project that was supposed to benefit veterans. Did Eleanor ever mention anything about collaborating with women for an art fair?"

Amanda scoffed. "Eleanor barely talked to me. She decided that since I wasn't sleeping around with everyone I saw, I must be jealous." Her lower lip trembled. "It's just hard. Mom and Dad died when she was sixteen, and I was only twenty-four. I tried to teach her how to take care of herself, but you know teenagers. She never wanted to listen. She always knew better. It didn't help that she looked like a damned swimsuit model. Men were *all over* her, and I mean all over. I remember she made a game once to see if she could date a different man every night for a month. She ended up having to turn men down because she was getting too many replies."

"We don't believe the killings were sexual in motivation," Faith said. "We're convinced it was connected to her work as an artist."

Amanda nodded. "Yeah. I can see that. Some people get really angry at artists."

"Did anyone get really angry at her?"

Amanda sighed. "Yeah, there was one guy. He got really pissed that she was doing some project or something for veterans. I guess she was making some watercolor portraits of soldiers and giving them to their families at a discount, and he had some issue with it because it was 'promoting war' or something. He wanted her to do another line of works celebrating symbols of peace like Fidel Castro, Che Guevara and—you'll like this one—Muammar Qaddafi. Fucking idiot. Do you think he killed her?"

"It fits the profile," Faith said, "that portion of it, at least. Did she ever tell you his name?"

"Briggs. I think it was a last name. She didn't give me any other name. She and I didn't talk much, but when we did, she would always complain about how Briggs was such an asshole and was always talking shit on her for doing work for the soldiers and what not. I asked her if he's such an asshole, why was she talking to him, and she said that she had to talk to Briggs because Briggs was big in the art world. She could fight with him, but she couldn't ignore him. Don't ask me how that makes sense."

"Did she ever seem afraid of this Briggs?"

"She said she was afraid that Briggs would make things difficult for her with the galleries. She wasn't worried about commercial work, but she wanted to do some fine art too, stuff that people would remember her for. She was afraid that Briggs would talk to people and poison her name. She was really relieved when the Mettifer Gallery picked up her Autumn collection."

"How did Briggs react?"

"They stopped talking after that. Eleanor promptly forgot about him. That was Eleanor. She lived from one day to the next and never thought about how what she did on Tuesday could come back to bite her on Saturday."

"We'll look into that," Faith said. "This is very helpful. Thank you."

"What would you have done?" Amanda asked out of nowhere. "If you were in my shoes. Would you have just left her alone to make her own choices, even if they were bad ones, or would you have told her that what she was doing was dangerous and that she was going to get herself hurt?"

Faith smiled compassionately at her. "I would have done the best I could. Just like you did."

"I know," Amanda said. "It's just not enough. It's never enough."

Turk trotted to her side and laid his head in her lap. Her lips trembled, and then she broke down, falling to her feet and holding Turk close while she wept.

Faith and Michael left the room and let Turk comfort her. Faith felt exhausted, but they had a new lead to follow up on now, so she also felt good.

In the back of her head, though, she feared that once more this lead would end up in the middle of nowhere.

"We'll have to establish a connection to the other victims," Michael said, evidently thinking the same thing.

"We have to find out who Briggs is first," Faith replied. "We've got an epidemic of people who hate their art but aren't responsible for killing them. A whole lot of fans, but no Mark David Chapmans."

"You said that, not me."

"It's true. Part of me is wondering if this doesn't have anything to do with art after all."

"We go where the evidence leads," Michael said. "Right now, the evidence leads to Briggs."

"The mysterious Briggs. Time to start digging through our victims' connections again."

"Maybe Lila Voss will know," Michael suggested, "and maybe we can tell her to call the police back and get some protection while she's at it."

"Stranger things have happened."

They tried Lila Voss at the number provided and got a voicemail that said, "If you're calling me, and I'm not picking up, it's because I'm at the ceramics convention. I won't be home until it's over, and I never answer my cell phone at work, so leave a message if you want, but I'm probably not going to answer for a while."

Faith looked at Michael, then said, "Hi, Lila, this is Special Agent Faith Bold with the FBI. I'm leaving a message for you because we have reason to believe that you're being targeted by a particularly violent serial killer. I'm sure you've gotten messages from the police department. They tell me you're not home, which is good, but they don't know where you are, which is bad. Please call us back and let me know you got our messages. We can offer you protection until we find the killer, but you have to call the police department back and tell them you want it. Also, we have questions to ask you that we think might help us find the person responsible for killing four other women you know."

She hung up and said, "Okay, now I'm worried. How long do these conventions last?"

Michael shook his head. "No idea."

She sighed. "You'd think she would at least call back. She could verify the number online and then return the call."

"You'd think people would have common sense," Michael agreed, "but they so rarely do."

Faith had to agree with him there. "All right. Well, let's see if we can find a Briggs."

"I'll go pick up some donuts and coffee. I have a feeling we're going to be here for a while again."

"Let's hope not too long. Lila's the only one left. I have a hunch our killer will be waiting for her when she gets home."

"I'll talk to the Chicago field office and make sure they keep watching her house. At the very least, we should catch anyone suspicious before it's too late."

"Good idea."

Faith got to work, struggling to remain calm. This anxiety always plagued her when she was nearing the end of the case. Things always seemed just a little more anxious then.

There was an extra sense of urgency this time, though. Lila was the only one left from the art fair project these five women had worked on. The killer would be feeling a sense of urgency to get this over with. That meant he might make mistakes, but it also meant they had a shorter clock to stop him.

It was a race to the finish line, and if Faith didn't win, then the prize would be pulling Lila Voss's charred corpse from an oven.

CHAPTER SEVENTEEN

The killer was excited. One left. One more, and then the killer could close the chapter on this whole deal with these women.

And what next? The killer still hadn't decided. Leaving the game was tempting. The police didn't seem to be anywhere near a conclusion, so it was quite possible the killer could just lay low until the case went cold and never risk harm or incarceration.

Then again, there were others out there who deserved to be brought to justice, others who had committed crimes worthy of death. The killer didn't think rest was possible. Not after this much success.

It could be done. They could be stopped. They could be punished. Maybe not enough to slow the machine down, but the killer could make a difference to a few.

The killer had worked through all the moral conundrums. No, it wouldn't bring any of the victims back. No, it wouldn't stop the war machine. No, it wouldn't make enough of a difference for history to remember it. What history would remember was a serial killer targeting artists, not an activist protesting violence by showing viscerally what violence bred.

Still, fewer people like these women would walk the Earth, and even if that fewer was such a minuscule difference as to be barely quantifiable, the killer would have the satisfaction of knowing they were gone.

One more. One more, and then who knows? Probably split the difference. Take some time off and look around for more people to hunt.

That thought brought the killer up short. Hunt? No, not hunt. That's not what this was about. This wasn't sport, even if it was challenging. This wasn't for fun, even if it was enjoyable. This was deadly serious and very sobering.

The killer paused a moment and reflected. That was one price that hadn't been considered yet. This would have an effect on the killer. It wouldn't leave the killer whole. Like so many jobs, this one would eat away and erode the killer's humanity. Over time, it could leave the killer scarred and calloused to the point where the reflection in the mirror was unfamiliar.

That was an argument in favor of stopping. How much more could the killer take before the killer became not an instrument of justice but of evil?

The killer was pulled from those thoughts when the last one walked in front of the crowd and smiled. Such an innocent, happy smile. Look at the little crocodile bare its teeth. Isn't it pretty?

The crocodile was gesturing and explaining something about ceramics. The gentle art of molding clay and shaping it before incinerating it, glazing it and incinerating it again.

Despite the killer's mockery, this art really was respectable. This was an appropriate use of fire to mold the environment to a purpose helpful to the race. Still, it was hard to separate the art from the artist when the art was used to celebrate the bringers of death.

The crocodile gestured to something behind a sheet, and of course, when the sheet was pulled off, it revealed a mural dedicated to those who murdered innocents.

And the crowd goes nuts. And everyone fucking cheers.

Yay! Look how she captured the details of those guns!

Dude, do you see how accurate that bomb is?

Man, I wish I could see a real airplane glass an entire city of civilians.

And the crocodile smiled, eyes circling the water as it regarded its prey.

Well, it would learn better. The killer would make sure of that.

One more. And she would meet her end tonight.

CHAPTER EIGHTEEN

Michael sighed and pushed away from his computer. "I need a break," he said. "I can't keep doing this crap."

Five hours of work had gotten them exactly halfway through the rest of the list with no Briggs, either first or last name. "We need to get some kind of database search tool where we can feed data into it and search for it without the information needing to be already stored in an existing database."

"I'm sure we can use some sort of client management software to do that," Michael replied. "I'll bring it up to the Boss when we get back."

"Better let me bring it up to him," Faith said. "He doesn't like you."

"Yeah, why is that? Anything I should know?"

"Not that he's told me. I assume it's because you're an annoying prick whenever you're around him."

Michael groused. "Yeah, I know. But in my defense, he's also an annoying prick."

"He's just straightlaced."

"I'm straightlaced, but I don't have a stick up my butt about it."

"Well, he has a whole field office to run. Not to mention the ongoing scandal of West and the fact that we've had our hands in every major serial killer case the nation has seen the past three years."

"Why are you making excuses for him? He's not any nicer to you than he is to me."

"I think he's a good SAC. He's hard to talk to, but he makes sure we have what we need to succeed, and best of all, he stays out of our way. I don't think you realize how amazing it is to have a boss who doesn't feel a need to meddle in everything you do."

"I think the word you're looking for is supervising."

"The word I'm looking for is tampering," Faith corrected. "The Boss doesn't do that, and that means that we get to do our jobs."

Michael sighed. "Well, as long as he doesn't try to fuck with my pension, I'm okay with that."

"I wouldn't worry about it too much."

"That's because you're a single woman with a dog. I have a wife to think about."

"Um, excuse me, not single. I have a boyfriend."

"Not the same."

She narrowed her eyes. "And why not?"

"You and David are casual. Ellie and I are committed."

"I'm committed!"

"I'm not saying you're going to sleep around on him or anything. I'm just saying he's right now for you. Ellie and I are forever."

She turned and looked squarely at him. "Where the hell is this coming from?"

He lifted a hand. "I'm not trying to fight. Forget I said anything."

"No, tell me. What makes you think I'm not serious about David?"

"Lack of sleep, lack of food and lack of caffeine. Let me correct two of those three problems now."

"You're not running away from this, Michael. Why did you say that David is just 'fun'?"

Michael sighed. "It's just… well, when I hear you talk about the future, you talk about you and Turk: where you guys are going to move, what you're going to do, whether Turk will like the Midwest or whether he'll miss the big city. I don't hear David mentioned once."

Faith blinked. She realized that she hadn't thought much about where David would fit in with all of that. When she did think about it, she just sort of… made herself stop thinking about it. "I… I mean, I hope he'll be around."

"Well, that's all I mean. You *hope* he'll be around. There's no question that Ellie will be around in my future because she *is* my future." Seeing Faith's expression, he said, "and it's okay if David isn't yours. You're both adults. You both have careers, you have different dreams for your futures. Maybe those dreams will include both of you, or maybe you'll enjoy what you have and part as friends. Either way is good."

Faith didn't answer, and Michael sighed. "Faith, I'm sorry. I didn't mean to make this awkward, really. I just made a stupid comment that I would never have made if I wasn't exhausted and frustrated and hungry. I'm going to go get us some donuts, sandwiches and coffee, and we'll get back to work finding the asshole murdering all these women, and we'll laugh at silly Michael and his stupid mouth."

Faith managed a smile, and Michael left to get the food. She intended to keep working while he was gone, but she found herself unable to focus after their conversation. She sighed and got to her feet, pacing around the room and trying to clear her head.

What *did* she want with David? She'd asked herself this question before, but she'd never followed it through to an answer. Anytime she got close to one, she pulled away and brushed the question off as something to deal with later.

But what did she want with him?

She liked him. That was true. He made her smile, he made her laugh, he made her feel comfortable being goofy and girly and flirty. She felt like she could be herself around him, the goofy side and also the driven, hard-boiled side that most men found intimidating. That was big. She didn't feel that way around most people, men or women.

He was hot. She was adult enough to admit that meant something. He was sexy, and he was good in bed, and that was also hard to find.

He was great with Turk, and that was probably the biggest thing he had going for himself. Turk absolutely loved him, and he was a good vet to Turk as well. Turk was probably the single creature that Faith loved most in this world, and having a boyfriend who loved him too was wonderful.

But did Faith love him?

She'd said she did every now and then, usually when it was clear in David's demeanor that he needed to hear her say it. She even believed it most of the time. What wasn't to love, after all?

But did she love him? If he died, would it devastate her? It was a morbid question to ask, but an important one.

Here was an even better one. If staying with David meant needing to stay in Philadelphia and not moving away to the quiet place in the country she dreamed of, would she stay?

That was a question she didn't have a good answer to.

She needed to deal with West. That was the great unknown that needed to be answered before anything about her future could be decided. She needed an answer to the West question before she could think about where David did or didn't fit.

Maybe when this was over, she would talk to the Boss about working on the West case after all.

She sat back down at her chair and continued to work through the list. As she sifted through names, she paid attention to other names that showed up more than once. So far, three names showed up in three women's contacts and eight showed up in two. No one showed up in all five but Jasper Flynn, and they had already cleared him as a suspect.

Well, there were still a lot of names to go. Odds are one or more of them would be connected to all five or at least all four of the current victims.

Faith recalled that it was at least somewhat possible that Lila Voss was the killer. She didn't look like she was big enough to strangle Sylvia Waters to death, but rage could make people accomplish things they otherwise couldn't, and if she got the drop on Sylvia, she could have had the ligature cinched up tight before Sylvia had a chance to do anything about it. It only took a few seconds for a blood choke to put someone unconscious.

Maybe instead of watching Lila's house, they should put an APB out for her.

The door opened, and Michael walked in, deftly balancing a box of donuts, a bag of sandwiches, and a drink carrier with two coffees. "Here you go," he said brightly, "a reason to forgive me for being an asshole."

Faith smiled and said, "Thank you, Michael. I forgive you."

He served her a half-sandwich, a donut and the coffee. "There's more food for later. I think we're probably going to pull another all-nighter."

"I hope not. Speaking of a related subject, I'm thinking we need to remember that Lila might also be the killer. I know it's a stretch to think that she's physically capable of this, but if there are only five women and four of them are dead, then either they're all targets—"

"Or one of them is the killer," Michael finished. "Good point. You want an APB out for her?"

"Yes. Tell Ricardo that she's a suspect. If nothing else, it might help us find her and put her under protection if she turns out to be innocent."

"That makes sense. Plus, it gives me a few more minutes to not stare at a computer screen."

"Don't milk it," Faith warned. "We still have a job to do."

"We always have a job to do. But I won't milk it."

Faith kept working while Michael talked to Ricardo. She found another name that was connected to three of the women—an editor from *Sculpture and Architecture* who had interviewed Marissa, Sylvia and Lila. No record of any connection to Cassandra or Eleanor, but she saved his name under the Possibles column.

Michael came back and said, "Okay. Got her where she needs to be."

"You found her?"

"No. Sorry. I mean, I told Ricardo, and he's putting the APB out."

"Wouldn't it have been simpler to just say that?"

"Yeah, but less fun."

"This was fun?"

He sighed. "It would be if you weren't such a square."

"Well, ha ha. There's your pity laugh. Now get to work."

They lapsed into comfortable silence while they worked. It occurred to Faith that she was more comfortable around Michael than anyone else. She was comfortable around David, but she also felt a weird pressure around him. Around Michael, there was no pressure. She could enjoy his company without feeling obligated for it to mean more.

That's what it was. She felt obligated to love David. He loved her so much that she felt like she had to return the feeling. That didn't necessarily mean her feelings weren't genuine, but they just seemed so much more forced. With Michael, she didn't have to worry. She could just be his best friend.

Oddly enough, she and Michael *had* dated for about a year. The relationship ended about a year before the Trammell case, which put it three and a half years before now. She had felt as strongly for him then as she did for David now and even believed for a moment that they would be together forever.

But back then, she had felt the same pressure, the same need to feel for him the way he felt for her. That was what ultimately broke them up. He wanted the relationship to move forward and began pushing for them to take steps like moving in together and talking about kids and a house and a wedding. She was too scared to commit—she thought at the time—and decided to pull away instead.

Maybe she just wasn't cut out for a long-term relationship. Maybe that was the real problem. She liked keeping people at arm's length. It wasn't that she hated people. She just needed her space, and when you were in a committed romantic relationship with someone, you couldn't expect to have the same kind of space.

That was why she and Michael were such good friends now. She could enjoy time with him, and when it came time for them to go to their separate lives, she could leave without feeling any guilt, and he could leave without feeling like he wasn't wanted. They had a perfect friendship that was perfect, as much for the distance between them as for the closeness.

She was pulled from her thoughts when Ricardo walked into the room. Faith saw his expression, and her heart sank. "Don't tell me you found Lila's body."

"No, not yet."

"Oh thank… wait. Not *yet?"*

"We put the APB out and got a call from the organizer of a ceramics convention in Milwaukee. A woman matching Lila Voss's description was seen struggling with someone who dragged her into a van."

"Man or woman?"

"Couldn't tell. Our witness only saw Lila, but she said it didn't look like Lila wanted to go with whoever took her. They also said that Lila was stumbling and looked drunk. They called the police in Milwaukee, and Milwaukee assumed it was just someone helping a drunk relative home. When they say the APB, they called us, just in case."

"How long ago was she taken?"

"Looks like two hours ago."

Faith swore. "Okay. We have FBI agents watching her house. Odds are the killer will take her there. If he does, then we'll jump on them. Get two officers there to help the FBI. Michael and I want to ride with you and oversee the APB. This has now become a manhunt."

"You mean woman hunt."

Faith stared hard at Ricardo. "Look me in my eyes and tell me if I'm in the mood."

"You're not in the mood. Sorry."

"Don't be sorry, be active. This is it. Night hasn't fallen yet. All the other murders were committed at night. We might still be able to catch this guy and save Lila's life."

"Lead the way, mon capitay."

Faith decided to let that one go. Despite her fear for Lila's life, excitement once more took over.

This was her element. This was what she did best.

I'm coming for you, Lila. Hang in there.

"Turk. Let's go catch a bad guy."

CHAPTER NINETEEN

The killer neared the house, but something in the back of the killer's head said the place was off. The killer frowned and scanned the area, wondering what could be causing the alert the killer felt.

The killer saw the stakeout vehicle three blocks away from the crocodile's house. It was a late-model panel van marked with a logo that read FRANK AND BARNEY PLUMBING.

Frank and Barney plumbing my ass. More like Federal and Bureau's Investigators.

The killer continued past the stakeout vehicle smoothly without so much as a glance toward the van. His back windows were tinted, but not enough to raise suspicion. They could see easily through the windows to the empty cab if they chose. They couldn't see below the windows to the woman tied up in between the second row and front row of seats.

Damn it.

DAMN it.

Damn IT!

What options did the killer have? Lila could always die a more conventional way—shot or stabbed—but the whole point was to kill her with her own tools. The whole point was to show that when you used your gifts to support death, death came to you.

The killer continued to the second to last right turn before the road ended, then turned right. This street would eventually connect him to a main street that would take them out of the subdivision. If the FBI vehicle followed them, the killer would park in front of one of the houses and leave the car as if they were parked in front of the killer's own house and pray that they wouldn't feel a need to loiter and watch him enter the home. If the FBI didn't follow, they would get back on the main road and then on the highway where the killer could think.

The FBI didn't follow.

The killer got onto the main road and headed for the highway.

Think.

Lila Voss needed to die in an oven. That was how you killed a potter. You burned them into a glaze like the glaze they put on ceramics.

Or…

Or…

The killer could bury her. That would work. Just like she shaped and hardened clay, she would be forced to become rigid and still. Concrete wasn't exactly clay, but the killer couldn't afford to be a chooser right now.

"Damn it. God damn it."

The killer spoke softly, but the last of the five heard the words anyway. She moaned, and the killer glared down at her. "Hush. If you want to survive, you'll keep quiet."

The crocodile quieted. She stared up at the killer with huge eyes.

The killer had told a lie, but it was a necessary one. The last thing the killer needed right now was for the crocodile to make trouble and attract attention. If he could hold out the carrot of survival long enough, maybe he could keep her quiet long enough to think.

The killer had concrete, loads of it remaining from the days of working for Hatfield Construction. No use had surfaced for it in the years since, but the killer had kept it around just in case. It seemed a need had surfaced.

The next question was where to take her. It would be a long process to bury her, at least a half a day. The killer would have to mix the concrete, dig a hole, place the crocodile inside and bury her, then wait at least fifteen minutes to ensure she hadn't somehow managed to escape and dig her way out. Finding a quiet enough place to do that in a metropolitan area of nine and a half million people was next to impossible.

The killer would have to do it in the backyard.

That was far from ideal. Plenty of people had been caught when their yards were dug up to reveal decomposing bodies. The killer would have to be careful. That meant a more complicated operation than just burying her under a slab of concrete. The killer would have to find a use for that space. Maybe a firepit or something. Something to justify the choice to spend hours digging a hole and filling it with concrete.

That didn't have to be decided immediately. The concrete wouldn't be ready to work on for at least a week. The crocodile could be dealt with, and then later, the killer could determine what justification could be used for the work.

At least the killer knew where to go now. Home was twenty-five minutes away. The killer would park in the garage, sedate the crocodile again, then get to work on the grave.

With the momentary panic of the FBI's presence dealt with, the killer smiled. Justice would still be served. The crocodile would still learn her lesson as the others had.

The crocodile moaned again, and the killer said, "Don't worry. I figured it out. It'll all be over soon."

CHAPTER TWENTY

"So no one got a description?" Faith asked.

"I'm afraid not," the convention center manager replied. "The only call we received was from another attendee who only saw the woman seeming to struggle briefly before being lifted into a van."

"So they saw her being lifted, but they didn't see who lifted her?"

"A pair of arms in a black jacket. They didn't actually see her placed into the van, but they saw her being lifted off the ground and when the van left, there was no one there, so it's reasonable to assume that she was taken. The caller was, I believe, nearly two hundred yards away from the van. That might explain why nothing else was seen in detail."

The owner, a fastidious looking man of around fifty with balding hair and a round, slightly jowled face, spoke with the practiced calm of someone who had spent a lifetime in middle management. The concern on his face seemed genuine, but the genteel affect infuriated Faith anyway.

Well, that wasn't his fault.

"And why was it that the police weren't notified as soon as you were?"

"It's my understanding the police were notified before me. The caller said they had spoken to the police but had waited to do so because they believe the woman was simply drunk and being helped home by a relative."

"And they could tell this from two hundred yards away?"

"The woman was clearly—"

"Can we call her by her name, please? It's Lila Voss."

The genteel middle manager at least had the decency to appear remorseful. "Of course. Miss Voss was stumbling and appeared to be unable to keep her feet. Miss Ramsey—that's the caller—believed that the person who carried her was simply helping her into the vehicle."

Faith sighed again. "Did you receive any complaints about anyone at the convention? Anyone being aggressive or suspicious or loitering anywhere?"

"Just the usual complaints of drug use and excessive drinking. Nothing out of the ordinary."

Faith nodded. "Okay. Thank you. If you think of anything else, please call me ASAP."

She handed him her card, then rejoined Michael. The frown on his face indicated that his conversation with Miss Ramsey didn't go any better.

"Didn't see anything. She was across the parking lot and stopped to watch a woman who appeared drunk possibly fight off someone who gently picked her up and helped her into a van. The individual was blocked from view by the van, so all she saw was a pair of arms in a jacket lift Lila and carry her behind the van, presumably placing her inside before driving away."

"She didn't see him walk around the front of the van to drive away?"

"No, she was loaded on the driver's side. It's a new model van. Most of them have doors on all four sides."

Faith swore. "What direction did the van leave?"

"South."

Faith nodded. "Okay. Did our buddies at Lila's house find anything?"

"Nothing physical. They're working on getting into the computer now."

"Okay. We're going to head back and join them. In the meantime, call Ricardo and put an APB out on the van. Bonus points if the owner of the van also has a four-wheel-drive SUV or truck."

"Will do."

She headed to the parking lot to see Turk sniffing around the space formerly occupied by their kidnapper. He had his nose to the ground and was gazing intently south.

"I know, Turk. We'll get him. We're on our way there now." Turk whined, and Faith added, "don't worry, boy. We'll find her."

She hoped she sounded more optimistic than she felt. They had rescued people at the last second many times, but it was always a near thing, and one of these days, they wouldn't make it in time.

The three of them sped back to Chicago. With their lights on and traffic relatively light, they covered the distance in an hour and a half, but that was already too much time. Marissa Stone had died instantly. Cassandra Holt had died in less than a minute. Sylvia Waters had taken the longest, possibly suffocating over the course of twenty or thirty minutes depending on how much oxygen was in the glass globe she was sealed inside. Eleanor Swift probably drowned within two or three. If Faith was right and the killer planned to burn Lila Voss alive, then it would take maybe an hour at the most to heat the kiln and toss her inside. Hell, Faith knew nothing about pottery kilns. For all she knew, it would reach lethal temperatures in minutes. Once Lila was inside, she wouldn't last long. Those ovens burned hot, Faith knew that much.

But she couldn't allow herself to think that way. Lila was the last one left. If she died, then the killer would have won. Even if they caught him, he would have one.

You can't handle that he beat you.

West's voice was an unwelcome intrusion into her thoughts, but she couldn't push it away.

Jethro Trammell won. He had you trapped, and there was absolutely nothing you could do about it. If it weren't for your Prince, you would have died there completely helpless. That's why you obsess over him.

West had never actually said those words to her, but it was the truth, the hardest truth Faith had to accept, and that was why she heard it in his voice. Jethro Trammell had beaten her, so she obsessed over him. West had beaten her, so she obsessed over West.

And you need to win, Faith. That is your greatest weakness. You need to win so badly that when you lose, you spiral utterly out of control.

He *had* said those words to her. Moments after beating her yet again, that time literally beating her and then stealing Turk.

And he was right. She needed to win. But not for the reasons West thought. He was so self-centered that he couldn't comprehend the fact that Faith needed to win not to pat herself on the back and say what a good girl she was but because she needed to keep innocent people safe. She couldn't accept that violent predators could prey on the innocent and get away with it.

But this killer had frustrated her in ways no other killer had besides West. They knew almost everything about this killer. They knew his motives, they knew his methods, they even knew his targets. But due to bad luck and clever planning on the part of the killer, they had been unable to stop him.

Faith wondered if he had saved these two for last because he knew that they would be out of town just when the police were trying to ensure their safety. It seemed ludicrous, but at the same time, it was almost miraculous that Eleanor Swift—the arrogant child who thought she didn't need anyone's help—and Lila Voss—the traveler who couldn't be bothered to answer her phone when she was working—would be the last two victims on his list.

It didn't matter. That was the worst of it. Lila Voss was gone. How she was taken was irrelevant. She was taken, and it was their job to get her back, no matter how clever their killer was.

Or to find her body.

When they reached Lila Voss's home, they found the place a circus. The two FBI agents assigned by the Chicago Field Office to watch the house had called four other agents, and Ricardo had sent a half-dozen officers. The place was crawling with people jostling, shouting and arguing for precedence. Faith would give them the benefit of the doubt and assume that they were well-meaning, but they weren't getting anything done squabbling like children.

She clapped her hands for attention, then shouted, "Everyone! We have a missing woman to find whose life is in imminent danger. We're not arguing anymore over who's in charge and who gets to do what. I'm in charge, and this is what each of you will do. Police, you report to Detective Ricardo. Your job is to find a late-model panel van with a driver's side rear door. The owner or renter of that van will also have a blue mid-size truck with oversized off-road tires. You will also be filtering any phone calls or emails with information on Lila Voss. FBI, you report to my partner, Special Agent Michael Prince. Your job is to look through every communication Lila Voss has made in the past year and find anyone with the name Briggs: first, last, middle or nickname. We suspect that Briggs is Voss's kidnapper and the serial killer responsible for the previous four murders. Hop to it!"

The formerly disorganized group immediately headed to complete their new jobs. Michael nodded approvingly and said, "The Boss would be proud."

Faith took a seat at Lila Voss's dining table and filtered the information the others brought to her. On the police side of things, it wasn't encouraging. Predictably, there were tens of thousands of panel vans registered in the Chicago and Milwaukee metropolitan areas. Surprisingly, there were hundreds of trucks that could fit the description. Opening it up to include half-tons brought that number to the high thousands. Blue was a popular color, apparently.

Most frustratingly, there were no individuals who owned both a blue off-road pickup and a panel van. Rental companies had records of individuals who had rented vans yesterday, but between Chicago and Milwaukee, that number still reached the hundreds. The situation was complicated by the fact that not only did the rental companies not have records of their customers' personal vehicles, but most of the panel vans were rented by companies, not individuals.

"Start with the individuals," Faith told the police. If we don't get a hit there, then we'll move on to the corporations."

Ricardo nodded, then sighed. "Damn it, this case is like a reverse onion. Everything we learn just brings us more questions than before."

"Don't give up, Detective," Faith said. "We've beaten odds bigger than this before."

"I'm not giving up," he assured her. "I'm just pissed."

"Yeah, me too."

The afternoon wore on into the evening. As night fell, Faith's anxiety grew. All of the victims had been killed at night. Faith suspected that was more due to the fact that the killer moved more easily at night than because of any ritualistic need to kill at night, but she realized now that part of her hoped that if they found Lila before nightfall, they might find her alive.

She didn't have that hope anymore.

Finally, just as the first stars appeared, Michael ran to her. "We found her!"

"You found Lila?"

"Well, I don't know yet, but we found Briggs."

"Briggs is a she?"

"Yep. Helen Briggs, reclusive and acerbic art collector extraordinaire. Also, possibly a serial killer."

Michael showed her a picture of a woman in her early forties with a toned physique and a serious, dare she say deadly, expression. "Address?"

"Ten minutes away."

"Good." She stood and called for attention again. "Okay! Police, I want you to keep looking for that van. FBI, you're with my partner and I. We're heading to a suspect's house. Police, we'll let you know if we find your van."

"I'm sending two officers with you," Ricardo said. "Just in case you need backup."

Faith doubted that a half dozen FBI agents and a K9 would need backup from two uniforms, but she understood that Ricardo's superiors would want this to be a Chicago PD collar or at least an assist. She really didn't give a rat's ass who got the credit, so she didn't argue. "Fine, but we're leaving now."

"Marco, Guillermo!" Rodney barked. "Go with them."

The makeshift task force left the house and jogged to their cars. Faith's heart pounded with a mixture of anxiety and anticipation.

They had found yet another suspect. Would this one lead them to Voss, or would this be another dead end?

CHAPTER TWENTY ONE

The light was still on in Helen Briggs' house when the team reached them. Helen heard the sirens and saw the lights and came out to see what was going on. When she saw eight armed men and women and a snarling German Shepherd charging her, she cried out and started to turn around.

"On the ground!" Faith shouted. "On the ground now, or my dog will put you there!"

"Oh, God!" Helen cried out. Fortunately for her, she did it while dropping to the ground. "What the hell is this?"

Turk leaped in front of her, snarling and barking. Helen shrieked and started to get up, but Faith dropped on top of her before she could.

"Give me your hands!" she shouted. "Right now!"

"Okay! God, what… what the hell is going on?"

Faith fixed the handcuffs and turned Helen's head to look at them. "Where is Lila Voss?"

"Lila Voss? What? I have no idea! I haven't seen her in over a month!"

"Back when you threatened her for promoting war?"

"What?" Helen's eyes narrowed suddenly. "I want a lawyer."

Faith glared. "If we find Lila Voss anything other than unharmed, it's going to go very badly for you. Where is she?"

"I don't know where she is. I'm not…" Helen's shifty eyes narrowed again. "Wait… this isn't about threatening her career?"

"This is about threatening her life. Tell us where the hell she is, or we'll find her, and when we do, I'll make sure that everything is as hard for you as it possibly can be."

"Okay, I had *nothing* to do with any disappearance. This is all a mistake."

"Then why did you text her saying she was, and I quote, 'an arrogant brat who would get what was coming to her, just like the rest of you veterans' art girls?'"

Helen's eyes narrowed again. She frowned and said, "I won't answer any questions without a lawyer present."

"That's fine," Faith said. "You'll get one."

She hauled Briggs to her feet and handed her to the officers. “Take her to the precinct. Michael, go with them. See if you can get her to talk. The rest of you, search the house.”

Faith and Turk followed the agents inside while Michael and the officers took Briggs away. As soon as Turk walked into the house, he began to bark loudly. He shot down the hallway and pawed at a door at the end of it.

Faith followed him and opened the door. It was a den, but instead of a tv and an easy chair, it contained an assortment of tools from various art professions. The tools were stacked on shelves with the larger ones placed on the floor. Each tool was labeled by the type of tool and the artist’s name. Among her collection, Helen had a paintbrush used by Picasso, a tripod owned by Ansel Adams, and a chisel used by Amedeo Modigliani.

One shelf contained a welding torch used by Marissa Stone, a piping bag used by Cassandra Holt, a blowpipe used by Sylvia Waters, a palette used by Eleanor Swift, and a carving tool used by Lila Voss.

***

“You can see why we might have trouble believing you.”

Helen Briggs sat across from Faith and Michael, her head lowered, and her lips thinned almost to the point of disappearing from her face. Her lawyer wore a similar expression and, like Briggs, refused to make eye contact with the agents.

Faith allowed the silence to continue a moment, then said, "The big problem here, Miss Briggs, is that the blowpipe was the one missing from Sylvia's house the night she was murdered. It’s the same one used to seal the glass in which Sylvia Waters was suffocated. Your fingerprints are all over it.”

“Of course my client’s fingerprints are all over it,” the lawyer, a shrewish-looking man of around Helen’s age named Walter Kent, replied. “She has the piece in her collection, voluntarily given by Miss Waters.”

“I would believe that, except that there’s a bit of glass on the tip of that pipe, and the police lab has confirmed that the glass is a high-silicate compound that is identical to the compound used to create the piece in which Miss Waters was suffocated.”

Kent scoffed. “So what? She used similar pipes for many of her creations.”

"No, she didn't. The type of glass she used is very durable and temperature-resistant. It requires special tools to be worked with properly." She tapped the blowpipe, which sat in an evidence bag on the table. "This tool. Most of Sylvia's creations didn't require such high-silica glass, so she used a more malleable low-silica compound that was much easier to work with and required less heavy-duty tools. In fact, the *only* item present at her studio that required this kind of high-silica glass was the globe."

"Miss Waters is known for many other creations," Kent replied. "No doubt my client received an earlier pipe from a different piece."

"Is that your story, Miss Briggs?" Faith asked.

"Before you answer," Michael said, "Know that you are under oath. You're required to speak only the truth, or you can be held accountable for perjury."

"Helen, don't answer that. This is ridiculous," the lawyer said, "we'll prove this in court. We don't need to haggle over evidence now. Present it to a jury, and we'll prove that this pipe came into Miss Brigg's possession before Miss Waters' death."

"Okay," Faith said. "We'll leave the question of the pipe aside for now. Miss Briggs, what kind of car do you drive?"

"Why?" Kent insisted.

"We're trying to see if she might have been near Miss Waters' home on the evening of her murder."

Kent scoffed. "I fail to see how placing Miss Briggs at the home of a business associate is supposed to implicate her in a murder."

"So there should be no reason for you to refrain from answering the question."

"All right." Kent stood. "You're fishing. We'll see you in court."

"Very well," Faith said, lifting her hands. "We'll be upfront. You drive a 2000 Land Rover Defender 110 with thirty-five inch off road tires. We know this because we matched the tire tracks leading from the forest behind Sylvia Waters' house to your vehicle. We confirmed that you were at her house the night she was murdered. I find it odd that you chose to park off the road behind her house rather than in front of her house, considering she was a business associate."

Kent sat slowly, his face pale.

"Yeah, we're not fishing," Michael said. "We have your client on the hook. We're trying to give her a chance to get off of the hook. I'll be honest, she's not doing a very good job."

Kent gathered himself and said, "There are many vehicles that match my client's car."

"Actually, there aren't. There are fewer than fifty 2000 Defender 110s with thirty-five-inch Yokohama mud-terrain tires that have the same exact suspension components and axles giving the same exact track. Only three of them are in the United States, and only one of them within a thousand miles of Chicago. That's the bitch about driving unique vehicles. When you use them to commit crimes, it's very easy to track you."

"Okay," Kent said, "we're done here."

"You are not done here," Faith said. "As my partner said, we aren't fishing. We have you at the home of one of our victims on the night of the murder and in possession of an item taken from that home the night of that murder. We have an established connection between you and all five of our victims. We have you making threats to one of our victims, who is currently missing."

"Were you in Milwaukee yesterday afternoon?" Michael asked.

"I'm sure you can verify that," Kent said. He stood again. "Helen?"

"We'll let you know when you can leave. You don't decide when this interview is over."

"You can't coerce my client into answering your questions."

"The police department can make her stay here and listen to them, even if she chooses not to answer."

"We have nothing more to say to you."

"Then shut up and let me finish asking my questions."

Kent sat down with a forced laugh. "We are going to tear you guys apart in court."

Michael smiled at Helen. "So, you've probably guessed already, but we can verify that you were in Milwaukee. Only you weren't driving the Land Rover. You were driving a rented Dodge panel van. It's rather unique because it has a sliding door on the driver's side as well as the passenger side."

"I was purchasing artwork," Helen explained.

"Helen, be quiet," Kent snapped. To the agents, he said, "There is nothing wrong at all with purchasing art from an art convention. You are trying to base this case on conjecture."

"No," Michael countered, "we're basing it on your client's presence at the scene of one victim's murder and another's kidnapping, and the criminal threats she made to another victim."

“We just want Lila back,” Faith said. “Just tell us where she is. We can work out a plea deal for you. We’ve done it before.”

“I didn’t kill anyone,” Helen said.

“Helen, be—” Kent began.

“Just hush for a moment, Walter.” Helen looked Faith in the eye. “I didn’t kill Lila. I didn’t kill anyone. Yes, I knew these women. They were friends of mine at one time. We fell out when they decided to pursue projects that featured veterans. I'm sorry to tell you this, but that's not in vogue these days. It's not popular to promote warfare, even in a benign way. I advised all of them to change their focus to something more appropriate for the times. Marissa was the only one who took my advice, but she still chose to pander to events designed to support the troops.”

“Must have been frustrating to see all of them succeed wildly after ignoring your advice,” Michael offered.

Faith held a hand up for quiet. “So why were you at Sylvia Waters’ house?”

Helen shrugged. “I wanted her blow pipe.”

“Helen!” Kent barked.

“Oh please, Walter, don’t be a fool. They have an ironclad case for serial murder, and you know it. If I’m honest with them, I’ll get a trespassing and theft charge and a failure to report. We can work that down to a fine and a commuted prison sentence.”

She looked at Faith and said, "I wanted her blowpipe. It's a unique model. As you said, most people don't work with that high-silicate glass. Sylvia was the only one in the country who did besides Veronica Chase, and between you and me, Veronica is stuck in the past. She thinks the more intricate a work is, the more artistic it is. That hasn’t been popular since Rembrandt. Wrong art, I know, but you get my point.

“I just wanted the pipe. I knew she’d never give it to me after we fought, so I went to her house to steal it. I didn’t expect her to be home. I thought she would be back the following day.”

She sighed. “Well, she was home. As for not reporting her death, I think that’s pretty obvious.”

“Of course. Why be inconvenienced by a theft charge over a little thing like the brutal murder of a woman?”

“Judge me if it makes you feel better,” Helen said, “but I’ve told you the truth. I wanted Sylvia’s blow pipe. I got it. Now I’ll pay the price for doing it the wrong way.”

Faith and Michael fell silent long enough that Kent said, "Okay. You got your answer. Are we done here?"

"I don't believe you," Michael said. "You went to a lot of trouble to steal that thing the way you did. Why not just park in front of her house? Like you said, she's a business associate. You had a legitimate reason to be there. Why not park in front of her house during the day, wait a couple of hours, then leave with the pipe? You weren't expecting her to be home."

"I didn't think of that," Helen said sourly. "I just… look, I never thought this would become such a big thing."

"The murder of four women is usually a pretty big thing," Faith opined.

"Yes, well, color me stupid. I suppose that's part of thinking only of myself."

"I don't appreciate the irony," Michael said. "Tell us where to find Lila, or we'll charge this as a federal case. That means capital punishment."

"That's coercion!" Kent shouted immediately.

"I don't know where she is! Helen insisted. "I didn't take her!"

Michael opened his mouth to retort again, but Faith stopped him and nodded to the corrections officer waiting by the door. "We're done for now. Miss Briggs, if you think of anything else we should know, tell your corrections officer to get a hold of us. Mr. Kent, for the time being, you can reach out to Chicago PD for the local and state charges. If any federal charges are pending, we'll notify you."

She led Michael outside, and as soon as they were out of earshot, Michael swore. "The nerve of that bitch. To sit there and look us in the eye and say she doesn't know where she is. We've got her for four murders. She displayed the murders in a way that suggests she wants people to see them. What harm will come to her by letting us see the fifth?"

Faith shook her head. "I'm not convinced she's our killer."

"What? Come on, Faith. She has the murder weapon from Sylvia Waters' place, we've placed her there on the night of the murder, she's made criminal threats against Eleanor Swift, and she was in a rented panel van at the convention where Lila Voss was taken."

"Yes, but she doesn't fit the profile. She's in good shape, but I can't see her knocking over Marissa's statue or overpowering Sylvia. She's acted suspicious, but only when she thought we were picking her up for theft. She was genuinely surprised when we told her that Lila was missing."

"She *seemed* genuinely surprised. Criminals do that. And I don't mean to be an asshole, Faith, but sometimes, you've been fooled by criminals putting on acts like that."

Faith stifled the hurt that comment gave her. "West is different, Michael."

"Not really. I'm not saying that he's not smarter and more capable than other criminals, but the basic idea is the same. We have evidence—real evidence—linking Helen Briggs to these murders. We can't let hunches overpower that."

Faith sighed. "She's not talking. If she is the killer, she's not going to give us Voss. If she's *not* the killer, then she might know something that can help us find her. Either way, talking to her again and trying to get more information can't hurt."

Michael sighed and shook his head. "All right. Because it's you, I'll play along. I still think this is a waste of time."

They headed back to the interview room and caught Helen just as they were leaving. "Miss Briggs!" Faith called. "Wait!"

Helen, Kent and the corrections officer turned around.

"Miss Briggs, I want to ask a few more questions."

"You can ask them another time," Kent answered. "I think you've asked quite enough for today."

"I'll give you the benefit of the doubt," Faith said. "You say you didn't murder those women. All right. For the purposes of this conversation, I'll agree with you. But I think you might know who did. Even if you don't think you do, I think you might. If you can help us find the person who really is responsible, it could go a long way for you. It would prove you're not the murderer. It could possibly even convince the police department to overlook the charges you currently face."

Helen looked at Kent. The lawyer frowned, and the two whispered to each other for a moment. Then Kent turned back to Faith. "All right. My client will hear your questions."

They returned to the interview room, and Faith got straight to the point. "You mentioned that they started focusing on veteran-themed work. Do you recall when exactly this change occurred?"

"Yes. About a year ago, they had an idea for an art fair to raise money for veterans. They were going to market it in a way to enhance their goodwill and increase their status as artists and professionals. It fell through because they started squabbling over money. Typical nonsense. I doubt it would have made them any money to begin with."

"Were you involved with this project at all?"

"At first. I tried hard to get them to consider making the beneficiaries something more socially acceptable, like children or sufferers of disease. They ignored me."

"When you were working on this project, do you recall anyone who opposed it vehemently for philosophical reasons?"

Helen laughed. "Several. Most of the people who knew about it fell into two camps: the God bless guns and America camp and the all soldiers are murderers camp."

"Did anyone in the second camp strike you as particularly suspicious?"

"Not really. They're all the same sort of person."

Faith felt frustration trying to creep to the forefront of her mind. "This person would have access to the victims. It would be someone who could reasonably know where they all live."

Helen frowned. "Hmm. Well, that does narrow it down. Besides myself and the boy who delivered their art supplies, I'm not sure who it could be. Possibly Alan."

Faith released the breath she was holding. "Wonderful. Tell me about Alan."

"Alan was an event manager who was going to promote the event for them. From what I heard, he visited each woman in turn trying to convince them—as I did—that the best way to succeed was to change the beneficiary to something people would buy into. When he was unsuccessful, he grew aggressive and threatening. This didn't stop until one of the women—Cassandra, I believe—threatened to go to the police."

Faith grinned. "Great. Does Alan have a last name?"

"Crosswell."

"And an address?"

"I'm sorry, agent. That's as much as I have for you."

"What about a description?"

She sighed. "Caucasian. Blue eyes, brown hair. Over six feet. Very muscular. Intense gaze. Attractive, if I'm being honest. He didn't show much interest in me, though. Not in any of the women. I assumed he wasn't interested in women."

Faith couldn't care less what Alan was or wasn't interested in. "Thank you, Miss Briggs. This is a huge help."

"I hope so. I don't look forward to a lengthy prison sentence."

"If you're telling me the truth, you won't."

She rushed from the room, Michael and Turk hot on her heels. They reached the conference room and quickly looked up Alan Crosswell.

A few seconds later, they got a hit. Alan Crosswell, forty-seven. A jack of all trades who had worked in fields as varying as public transportation, construction, plumbing and event promotion. He was now officially listed as retired, but he had filed for a new driver license two months ago, so his address was stil current.

And about thirty minutes away.

"All right, Turk," Faith said. "For real this time: let's go catch a bad guy."

CHAPTER TWENTY TWO

The killer slumped into a chair and breathed deeply. The grave was finished, but it had taken all of the killer's energy. The burial would have to wait until some of that energy returned.

Still, the killer was in good spirits. It had taken only an hour to prepare enough concrete and start it mixing and only six to dig the graves. That was much better than the twelve hours anticipated.

The crocodile stirred and moaned. The sedative was wearing off again. The killer wouldn't bother injecting her again. They were nearly half a mile from anyone else, and even if she was conscious, she would be in no shape to scream for a while yet. The killer would recover much faster than she would.

The crocodile turned her face to the killer, and her eyes widened. "Alan?"

The killer smiled at her. "I'm surprised you remember me."

"Alan? Where… what…" her eyes widened further. "It's you?"

"It's me."

The crocodile pushed forward in what Alan assumed was an attempt to regain her feet. It worked about as well as she could expect, in other words, not at all. She pitched forward and hit her head on the concrete floor. She lay still long enough that Alan decided she had knocked herself unconscious.

Then she started to cry. Her chest hitched, and tears rolled down her cheeks. "Oh no. Oh God."

"Well, you were the one trying to run," Alan said. "What did you think was going to happen?"

"Why?" she asked. "Why are you doing this?"

Alan felt a rush of anger at the question. Why would she ask why? Wasn't it obvious? Was she literally so blind that she couldn't even conceive of the possibility of someone wanting to punish her for her heinous beliefs?

Then again, murderers and those who supported them often were blind. Just another reason why they shouldn't be allowed to exist.

Instead of shouting at her like he wanted, Alan shifted in his chair and stared at her. His lips smiled, but his eyes were as cold as the ground where minutes from now, the crocodile would rest for eternity.

"Let me tell you a story," he said. "You've heard it before. Odds are you've never paid attention before now, but there's a first time for everything.

"There's a kid. He's a good kid. Most kids are. He's not a perfect kid. Most kids aren't. He lives with his mother and father in a small home amidst a lot of other small homes in a good neighborhood filled with mostly good people who are just doing their best to get by.

"Or so the kid believes."

Alan paused and took a moment to process the rush of emotion that came from discussing these events. Even now, over thirty years later, the wounds were still fresh.

"That child's father is a soldier. A good one. A sergeant major. Most soldiers don't get to be sergeant majors. It takes over twenty years to become a sergeant major. It took this child's father twenty-two.

"That child still remembers the day his father becomes a sergeant major. It's a good day. His family is so proud of him. His wife—the child's mother—flirts with him and teases him the way she used to do when the child was very young. The child isn't grossed out by this. He's happy. His father is a good man.

A year later, the sergeant major has to go away. It isn't the first time he's had to go away, but this time is different. This time, he's going away somewhere the child and his mother can't visit him. There's a war, and one of the allies of the country the sergeant major serves is in trouble. So he's going to help protect them. He'll be gone for a year or so, then he'll be back. It won't be too much trouble. The enemy they're fighting isn't very strong. There's nothing to worry about."

Alan paused again, squeezing his hands rhythmically a few times to calm the anger he feels. When he was calm, he looked back at the crocodile.

"The sergeant major doesn't come home. The enemy isn't as weak as they think. The sergeant major's army wins the war, but the sergeant major doesn't come home. Instead, a flag comes home, neatly folded and placed in a walnut wood case with glass over the top. The sergeant major's dog tags are brought home as well. There's a chunk missing from one of them where a machine gun bullet glanced off of it before shredding the sergeant major's left lung, heart, stomach and left kidney before leaving his body."

The crocodile sobbed again, rolling over onto her back.

"It is sad," Alan agreed. "The child was very sad. So was the child's mother. So sad, in fact, that she stopped speaking to the child. She stopped looking at him. Stopped touching him, stopped holding him, stopped telling him that she loved him. I think she saw the sergeant major in the child, and the sight was too painful for her to accept. I'm not sure.

"Anyway, the child's mother decided that since she didn't have a sergeant major to keep her warm anymore, she would use rye whiskey instead. Always Tennessee malt, never Kentucky or Virginia or any other state. Tennessee rye was the sergeant major's favorite.

"So, she keeps herself warm for a while, but she doesn't know that the rye whiskey that keeps her warm is poison. Or she does, but she doesn't care. She's not strong like the sergeant major. She can't stop.

"So, she drinks and drinks and drinks, and when the child is a few days away from becoming an adult, he finds his mother face down at the foot of the stairs. She fell the night before and snapped her neck. The child finds her in a pool of blood and vomit."

"Oh God," the crocodile said, "Alan, I'm sorry. I'm so sorry."

"Me too," Alan said. "I'm very sorry. I don't know that I believe that you're sorry, but I appreciate the sentiment even if fear is the only thing that prompts it.

"Anyway, the child does what he has to do. He buries his mother, goes through the process of handling her estate. He's asked if he wants to keep the house, but he doesn't. He wants to move somewhere far away where he can forget.

"He doesn't forget."

Alan paused again and thought of the parallel between his mother's body and that of the baker. He didn't get to see the baker firsthand, only saw the pictures when they were leaked online. He wishes now that he had stayed to watch.

"He leads a good life. He marries a good woman. He doesn't have children because his wife can't carry them, but that's okay. He loves her. He has a good job building things, using his hands to create rather than destroy. He's happy.

"But he remembers. He always remembers. And as the years go by, and he grows older—older than the sergeant major ever got to be—the memories get stronger. They poison everything until all he can see is that deformed dog tag and his mother's broken corpse.

“So he leaves his wife. She doesn’t want him to. She still loves him even if he’s angry now and not the happy man he once was. The child feels bad because he loves her too, but he can’t be there for her anymore.

“So, he lets her go and lives alone. He leaves his job and tries a few others, but none of them drive away the memories. He starts to think, and when he starts to think, he starts to realize.”

Alan stared directly into the crocodile’s eyes now. She may have felt no true emotion when she was profiting off of death, but she feels it now. The terror in her eyes shows it.

“He realizes that the sergeant major was not a good man. This is a hard realization for him. For a while, he becomes well acquainted with liquor—not rye, not the drink of the sergeant major and the absent mother—but vodka. Clear, flavorless, harsh and biting. He drinks it, thinking maybe he’ll follow his mother away, but then he thinks some more.

“Was the sergeant major really a bad man, or was he just led astray by a world that celebrates death and violence? Perhaps, if the world would learn to focus on things that build and people that create and not things that demolish and people that destroy, there would be fewer children looking at a folded flag and shattered dog tags and more children holding their fathers.

“The child isn’t a fool. What is one man going to do in the face of thousands of years celebrating death? Nothing. Not a damned thing. When the child dies, the world will still be full of people who kill and people who celebrate killing.

"But the child can know. He can know that he did his best, meaningless though it is. He can know that at least some people suffered because they supported evil.”

He took a deep breath and released it slowly. “It’s not personal. I guess I’m just now realizing that. I don’t hate you personally. I didn’t hate any of the others personally. I thought I did, but now that I’m talking through it, I realize I don’t. I just hate what you stand for. I picked you guys because your memories were fresh in my mind from when I implored you to dedicate your creation to something other than the service of destruction.”

The crocodile released a choking sob. “I’m sorry. Please. Please don’t kill me. I didn’t mean it.”

“It doesn’t matter. You did it. You were warned not to, and you did. You’re not innocent.”

"Please. I'll do whatever you ask. I'll pull my work from the city mural. I'll never make anything about soldiers or veterans ever again."

"I know."

"No! Please!"

Alan stood and breathed a heavy sigh. "I'll have to put you out again. Thank you for listening."

He grabbed a needle and stepped closer to the crocodile as the crocodile begged and squirmed.

"Hush now," he said, gently pressing the needle into her neck. "It'll be over soon."

CHAPTER TWENTY THREE

It was after ten o'clock when the police and FBI team arrived at Alan Crosswell's home in Palos Park just southwest of Chicago. There was a light on in Alan's garage, and when Faith saw the van parked in the driveway, her heart leaped.

She pressed the call button on her radio and said, "Follow my lead. I'm going to send Turk ahead. He'll reach the killer before we do."

"We'll be right behind you," Ricardo promised.

"You don't want to wait until we're sure he's not armed?" Michael asked. "What if he shoots Turk?"

"I won't let Turk get too far ahead. I just want him up front so he can lead us directly to the killer."

"Good point."

They parked in front of the driveway and rushed forward. Alan's home sat on top of a small hill that bordered the Cherry Hill Woods nature preserve. That left them with no chance of taking him by surprise.

So they chose speed instead. Turk ran ahead of the group, barking and snarling. Turk and Michael were just behind, guns drawn and cocked. A few yards behind them were Ricardo and a half dozen Chicago PD officers and behind them, the four FBI agents loaned to Faith and Michael by the Chicago Field Office. Twelve armed law enforcement officers and one badass K9. That should be enough.

Turk ran straight to the garage, snarling and pawing at the door. Faith quickly determined that the front door and window would be the best way in.

"We brought a ram," Ricardo said, pointing to Marco, who held the thick metal bar in one heavily muscled hand.

Faith nodded and stepped aside so Marco could take center position. Turk stood next to her, tail switching back and forth as he prepared to rescue Lila.

Faith desperately hoped she was still there to rescue.

Ricardo knocked on the door. "Chicago Police! We're here with the FBI! If you're in there, Alan, this is your one chance to come out without getting hurt! Keep your hands where we can see them and come out slowly and quietly, and we can do this the easy way. Don't make us come in after you. This door opens any other way than you opening it and voluntarily surrendering, and it's not going to be good for you!"

No answer.

Ricardo knocked one more time. "Alan! It's now or never, buddy. You have ten seconds, and I'm not going to count them out loud, so get your ass out here now!"

No response.

Ricardo waited exactly ten seconds, then nodded to Marco and stepped aside. Marco squared his hips, then torqued his shoulders and slammed the ram into the door. Faith heard wood splinter as the entire right side of the jamb split. A second strike with the ram burst the door open.

"Go, Turk!"

Turk immediately sprinted through the officers, growling and barking. Ricardo, Marco, Faith and Michael rushed inside. The other four officers fanned out around the perimeter of the house in case Alan tried to flee out the side, and the four FBI agents rushed toward the rear of the house.

Turk led them to the garage. It was empty, but there was a syringe on a workbench and a vial right next to it that had recently been opened.

Turk ran to that vial and then to a spot on the floor a few yards away next to the wall. He looked at Faith and barked.

Lila Voss was here, and so was Alan. That was good news because it meant they were on the right track and finally hunting the right killer. It was bad news because they weren't there now.

"Damn it," Ricardo said. He spoke into his radio. "The garage is empty. We're going to clear the house. Look around the property for any sign of Crosswell or Lila Voss."

He put his radio down and looked at Faith. "Take your dog and go hunting. We'll clear the house."

Faith nodded and called for Turk. Turk ran past her and left through the back door. Faith kept pace, moving as fast as she could. Michael was panting heavily but he managed to stay within a few yards of Faith as they followed Turk around the house.

When they arrived behind the house, Faith saw the backyard was much larger than she expected. The fence extended to the crest of the hill and onto the other side. As Faith ran after Turk, the FBI agents from the Chicago office left a woodshed. Faith looked at them and they shook their heads.

"Then follow us!" she commanded.

Turk led them to the top of the hill, and when Faith heard barking, she knew they were on the right track.

"Get him, Turk!" she shouted. "Get him boy!"

She reached the top of the hill a moment later and saw Turk barking and growling at two figures standing next to a tractor pulling a concrete mixer and a hole about six feet long and three feet wide. Alan's plan became clear. He was going to bury Lila alive.

Lila was bound and apparently sedated. Her head lolled around, and her speech was slurred. Alan held her with one arm and pressed a gun to her temple with the other hand. He kept Lila in between himself and Turk, keeping the dog at bay.

Faith, Michael, and the other agents leveled their weapons at Alan and proceeded slowly forward. Alan glared at them and said, "One more step, and I'll kill her!"

The agents stopped. Faith guessed the distance at about thirty yards. She could make that shot easily, but not with a hostage in between her and her target.

"We need to get Lila out of the way," Michael whispered. "We have a shot if that happens."

Faith considered telling Turk to pull Lila down, but they risked Alan shooting Lila before Turk could clear their own shot. She would have to try to de-escalate the situation.

"Listen, Alan," she said. "You don't want to do this."

"Yes, I do. I did it to the other four, and I'm doing it to her. This is exactly what I want to do."

"No, it isn't. Think about this. Why are you killing these women?"

"Because they support murderers! They support people who go around killing innocents! They don't deserve to live!"

"I understand where you're coming from," Faith said. "Trust me. It's my job to hunt murderers. I know how infuriating it is to see people get away with those crimes."

"And yet here you are about to arrest me for punishing them!"

"Who did she kill, Alan? Lila Voss, the woman you're holding in your hands, who did she kill?"

Alan blinked. "She supported killers."

"She didn't kill anyone, Alan. Why go after her? Why go after someone who's never killed anyone? There are many soldiers in

Chicago, many veterans. Plenty of people who have killed others in combat. So why target her? Why target an artist who creates for a living?"

Alan's expression faltered. She was getting through to him.

"You don't want to do this. This won't change anything. It won't even change a little something. It would be like killing a line worker for Toyota because some people drive drunk and hit people with their cars."

Alan lowered his eyes, and the agents took advantage of that and slowly closed the distance. Faith pointed at Turk, then pointed at Lila's feet. Turk took a step, and she held up her hand, then pointed at her ears. *Wait and listen for my command.*

Alan raised his eyes and everyone froze in place. "I have to do something," he said, softly enough that she nearly didn't hear him.

"This isn't the thing to do. You've killed people, Alan. You understand? You've become a murderer."

Alan's lip trembled. He looked down at Turk, who watched him warily, waiting for Faith's signal. He looked back at the agents, their weapons aimed steadily his way.

His arms relaxed, and for a moment, he looked like he might give her up. Then his eyes hardened. He looked at Faith and said, "So be it."

His arms started to tense again, and Faith had no choice. "Now, Turk!"

Turk launched forward, grabbing Lila's ankle and yanking down. Alan didn't react in time, and the gunshot he fired sailed harmlessly into the woods.

The agents fired. Alan jerked as three of the six rounds fired entered his torso. He dropped his weapon and stumbled backward.

"Hold your fire!" Faith called. "Enough!"

She ran ahead to Alan while Turk dragged the barely conscious Lila to safety. He sank to his knees, and she caught him just before he fell.

He looked up at her. His face was placid, and his eyes were filled with grief. Faith braced herself for the heartfelt dying confession he was sure to make.

"I hate all of you."

Those were the last words of Alan Theodore Crosswell.

***

"She'll have a long road to recovery. The barbiturates he used to keep her sedated were poorly dosed, so there's some long-term liver damage. Possibly permanent. A lot will depend on how she responds to treatment."

Faith nodded at the doctor. "Can I see her?"

"Sure. She's still a little groggy, but she did say she wanted a chance to thank the woman who saved her life." He looked down at Turk. "I'm normally supposed to say dogs aren't allowed, but I think I'll make an exception for Mr. Turk."

Turk nodded soberly, and the doctor chuckled. "I had a Shepherd myself when I was a kid. Named him Rooster. My Dad had a boot camp buddy in Vietnam named Rooster. The guy was separated from his team and ended up having to walk through enemy territory for eleven days evading Viet Cong patrols and fighting his way through NVA ambushes to get to safety. But he made it. Dad found Rooster in the woods back where we live all torn up from fighting with bears, cougars and wolves, but the dog made it." She reddened a little and said, "Anyway, I'll let you go see Miss Voss. Just reminded me of the good old days seeing another old war veteran like Rooster."

She ruffled Turk's fur, then stepped aside so Faith and Turk could go into the room. Lila smiled when she saw the two of them and sat up a little straighter. She looked better than she did at Alan's home, but the dark circles under her eyes and the pallor on her skin spoke of the long road she had ahead.

"Hey there," she said softly, her words slurring a little. "Guess I owe you guys some thanks."

Faith smiled. "Just doing our jobs, ma'am."

"Call me Lila. And it's a good job you two do. Where's your partner?"

"He's wrapping up some paperwork back at the Chicago Field Office."

Lila laughed. "Yeah, I imagine there's going to be a lot of that. That's why I found a career in art. Not a fan of paperwork."

"No one is."

Turk trotted up to her, and Lila grinned. "Hey, buddy!"

Turk jumped up and planted his paws on the bed so Lila could hug him. "Thank you. You saved my life. You're a good dog."

"He is," Faith agreed. "The best."

Lila pulled away and beamed at Turk. "And so handsome too. I bet all the girls at the dog park can't keep their paws off of you."

Faith wouldn't have believed a dog could blush before, but she would swear that Turk reddened at that.

He laid his head on Lila's lap so she could stroke his fur while she and Faith talked. Faith approached the bed and laid a hand on Lila's shoulder. "How are you feeling?"

"Tired. Sore. Washed out. Doc says that's because of my liver. They're going to give me some medicine that will help, but I'm going to have to go on a diet for the next fifteen years or so."

"Well, you picked the right time for it. They can make oat milk brownies now that taste exactly like the real thing."

Lila laughed, and Faith joined her. "Oh man," Lila said. "That's a good one. Just for you, I'll enjoy an oat milk brownie every Saturday morning. I'll even pretend you're not lying about it tasting like the real thing."

"I'll hold you to that."

Lila's smile faded. "So he got everyone else, huh?"

Faith's smile followed suit. "You don't need to worry about any of that. Your job is to make sure he doesn't get you. Any part of you. You get better, and you go back to work, and you make as many murals of veterans as you want. There's a lot more people out there like you than like him. Speaking of, the VA wanted me to let you know that they're covering one hundred percent of the cost of your treatment."

Lila's eyes widened. "Really?"

"Really. They wanted you to know that they appreciate everything you've done to raise awareness for combat veterans, and that they're available if you need anything. They've even offered to take over your ongoing treatment and cover you under a special dispensation for friends of veterans."

Lila smiled briefly, but it faded quickly, and fresh tears came to her eyes. "I wasn't doing it for veterans. I was doing it for myself. I just wanted the clout and the money, and veterans were an easy cause. None of what I did was especially good. A high school class could have done it."

Faith thought of her answer for a moment, then said, "You know what? It doesn't matter why you did it. A lot of people might not agree with that, but it really doesn't matter. Your work has helped a lot of people. There are veterans who felt alone in the world who don't feel alone because of that mural you put up in Lincoln Park. There are children now who will play there and feel a swell of pride because someone else remembers what their mommies and daddies did and feels grateful to them for it. Maybe you aren't an altruist, and maybe you didn't do it pro bono, but you did it. That's more than most people do, and it's enough for the people who are going to fight through another day of bad memories because of what you gave back to the world."

Lila smiled again, and this time it stayed. "Why do you do it?" she asked. "Catch criminals, I mean?"

Faith squeezed Lila's shoulder again. "So that people like you can keep doing what you do."

Lila's smile widened. Then her eyelids drooped.

"I'll let you rest now," Faith said. "But I'll be paying attention. I expect to be blown away by the next Lila Voss mosaic."

Lila gave her a thumbs up. "Count on it."

Faith and Turk left Lila in her room. On their way outside, Michael texted her. *Gonna get the rest forwarded to Philadelphia. Let's go home.*

Faith smiled and texted back. *One more Dave's donut before we go?*

A second later, her phone buzzed. *Aw hell. You talked me into it. See you there.*

Faith laughed and looked at Turk. "What do you say, Turk? Want to go catch a maple bar?"

Turk cocked his head in confusion. Faith laughed again and scratched him behind his ears. "Good boy."

CHAPTER TWENTY FOUR

"And then he said, 'I hate you all.'"

"Jesus. I'm sorry, babe."

Faith didn't particularly like when David called her babe, but she let it go this time. It felt good to be doing something other than worrying about West or chasing a murderer. Dinners like these were what made her wonder if maybe she could have a future with him.

"It's all right," she said. "It's not like I value the affection of a serial killer. I just…"

David waited patiently for her to gather her thoughts. That was another thing she loved about him.

"I just hate that he was lost so young. I looked him up on the flight home. His father was a medal of honor winner in the Gulf War. Held off a Republican Guard ambush long enough for his company to escape. Not quite long enough to make it until they came back with a squadron of gunships. Mom ended up killing herself, falling down the stairs drunk off her ass a week before he turned eighteen."

"Damn. That's awful."

"Yeah, it is." She pushed the remains of her tiramisu around her plate and said, "The worst part is that he seemed fine. He *was* fine. For at least twenty-five years, he did okay. Went to trade school, learned construction, made it all the way to project manager for a homebuilder in Chicago. Got married and by all accounts was a loving husband. Then, five years ago, he turned forty-two and just imploded."

"Mid-life crisis gone bad?"

She shook her head. "No, I don't think so. His father died at forty-one."

"Ah."

"Yeah. I think he'd been holding onto anger over that for a long time, and it just all came to a head. He left his wife, left his job and worked a few menial jobs for a while. Then last year, he managed to get his shit together. That's when he meets our victims and decides he's going to pick them to take his rage out on."

"It's a sad story. Sometimes people just turn rotten."

"That's what scares me," Faith said. "I don't know if people turn rotten or if they're always rotten, and no one knows it until it's too late. I think Alan Crosswell lived with this hate for thirty years before he acted on it. He hid it behind a veneer of happiness, but inside, he was just festering and festering. No one would have looked at him and predicted that one day he would brutally murder four women for no other reason than that he happened to run into them when they were working on an art fair for veterans."

"Hey," David placed his hand over hers. "There's more of us than there are of them. Your job forces you to interact with the worst of the worst, but most people aren't like that. Plenty of people lose their parents in war and don't turn into freak shows. Plenty of people suffer tragedy and don't feel a need to force that tragedy to be someone else's problem. Don't let these evil people you capture poison your faith in humanity. Remember, it's not about Alan Crosswell or Kenneth Langeveldt or Franklin West. It's about Lila Voss and all the other Lila Vosses who get a chance at life again thanks to the work you do. That's why you go to work in the morning. That's why you're a badass FBI agent." He leaned forward and kissed her softly. "And that's why I love you."

She smiled at him. "Thank you, David. I love you too."

She felt the usual pang of worry whenever she said those words, but she decided not to focus on them.

He started to pull away, but she put her hand behind his neck and deepened their kiss. His breathing grew heavier, and she came around the table, still kissing him, and straddled his lap. After a moment, he laughed into their kiss and picked her up, then carried her to the bedroom.

One day, she would have to decide when and if their connection would end. But not right now. Right now, she was happy, and that was all that mattered.

***

"You sure you can't stay?"

Faith smiled and kissed the tip of David's nose. "Not tonight. I have to get up early in the morning and run."

"You can run here. Huckleberry Road leads right to the same park you take Turk to every morning. You can even run home if you want."

She laughed. "And what about my car?"

"Well, you can run right back here and maybe stay a while."

She sighed and kissed him again. "Another night."

"When might that other night arrive?"

He kept his tone light, but his eyes showed his sadness and his concern. She felt a pang of guilt and said, "Soon. I just need to take care of a few things first."

"West?"

She looked away, and he sighed. "No, it's okay. I get it. I know it was hard for you to see what he did to me."

"It's not that, David. It's…"

She struggled to think of something to say, and David said, "Yes, it is. And that's okay. You wouldn't be Faith Bold if you didn't obsess over protecting everyone you love. Go home and sleep in your cold, empty bed."

She rolled her eyes and shoved him playfully. He laughed and lifted his hands. "Hey, I'm just saying."

"Goodbye, David. Asshole."

"Goodbye, Faith. Bitch."

"You get that *one*, Buster," Faith said with a smile. "But only because I started it."

"I think you started it earlier too, didn't you?"

She rolled her eyes and started to dress. "Yes, I did, and I hope you enjoyed it because if you're going to throw it in my face, it'll be the last time I start anything."

"I'm not throwing it in your face. I'm just happy. It's not every day that the woman initiates sex."

"You're walking on thin ice, Dr. Friedman."

"I am," he admitted. "But I'm moving too fast to stop. How can I gracefully extricate myself from this conversation."

She leaned down and kissed him. "You can stop talking," she suggested.

He made a zipping motion over his lips, and she laughed. "I'll see you later, David." As she left the bedroom, she looked over her shoulder and said, "Make me some tiramisu tomorrow night, and I might initiate again."

"My lady, you shall have the finest tiramisu this world has ever seen."

She laughed again and waggled her fingers at him.

Turk was unhappy about being woken, and let Faith know with a sullen glare.

"Yeah, I know. I'll give you an extra treat when we get home, okay?"

Turk grumbled but followed her to the car without further protest.

Faith started the old Windsor V-8 and smiled as the engine rumbled to life. She could understand the appeal of the quieter and more powerful engines in modern cars, but nothing could replace the sound of an old V-8 motor. She enjoyed the rumble for a minute, then headed home.

The moon was new tonight, and a slight fog settled over the road as she drove. This made her feel vaguely uneasy, but she wasn't sure why.

The unease didn't last for long. She didn't have a lot to feel uneasy about right now. She had solved a case, rescued an innocent woman, enjoyed wonderful dinner and dessert (and *"dessert"*) with her boyfriend and was now on her way home with the best dog a girl could have.

True, West was still out there, and there was at least a chance some mouth breather on his payroll would be waiting to learn that he had screwed up letting the nerdy-looking man in the stupid wool vest convince him to mug an FBI agent, but Faith was in good spirits. She was sure that whoever was waiting for her, if anyone, she could handle it.

She reached her door and went through the lengthy process of unlocking everything. The app for the electronic barricade took a few minutes to load, and she sighed impatiently and wondered if the damned thing was even worth it. Maybe she would just get a few manual barricade bars and just leave them off when she left the house. It wasn't like she kept valuables here she had to worry about, and after West's last visit, Turk went everywhere with her, so it wasn't really the end of the world if someone trashed her apartment.

She realized she had forgotten to remind David about getting a barricade for himself. She sighed, partly out of frustration for forgetting, and partly out of anticipation of the argument that would no doubt ensue when she brought it up. Even after nearly dying at West's hands, David was remarkably stubborn when it came to protecting himself.

Well, maybe she would talk to him after "dessert" tomorrow night. Sweeten the deal a little.

The app finally loaded and reassured her that the electric barricade was indeed in place. She pressed DISARM and heard clicks and a soft whirring as the upper and lower beams retracted from the floor and ceiling. Two key turns later, she had unlocked the latch and the deadbolt and opened the door.

The apartment was exactly as she had left it, and Faith breathed a sigh of relief. She didn't know how long this little one-bedroom would be her home, but it was her home for now, and there was a lovely sense of completion to walking into the compact living room and even more compact kitchen.

She switched on the tv. "Gonna be game shows for now, Turk," she said. "I'll put something better on in a minute."

She headed to her bedroom and changed. She had gone straight to David's place after the debriefing with the Boss, so she had worn her uniform. She usually did after a case. David liked the way she looked in it, and she liked the way he looked at her when she wore it.

Now that she was home, she ditched the tight dark khakis and equally form-fitting button-down in favor of a t-shirt and sweatpants. Sexy? No. Comfortable? Hell yes.

I have to remember to pack some of these tomorrow.

She smiled as she realized that she had just tacitly admitted to herself that she would spend the night with David tomorrow.

"Oh, what the hell? He's been a good boy. He deserves a sleepover."

She turned and headed for the door to return to the living room. Turk was standing in the doorway, looking intensely over her shoulder. The hair on the back of her neck stood up, and a moment later, a familiar voice said, "Well, well, well. Who do we have here?"

CHAPTER TWENTY FIVE

Faith's gun was on the bed, four feet behind her. If she could turn and lunge at the same time, she could have it in her hand in about one second. Then she could find the source of the voice and fire. She estimated another two seconds for that.

Three seconds. That was too long. West was too sharp for that.

"I'm sure you've thought better about trying to shoot me," West said, "so instead, why don't you turn around slowly, and we can talk?"

Turk growled and stepped forward, but he stopped a moment later.

"Smart dog," West said. "Did you teach him to recognize guns?"

Faith turned around slowly and saw West standing on the other side of her bed. He held her gun in his left hand, pointed at Turk. In his right hand was what looked to Faith like a Sig P226. In fact, it looked like the Sig P226 that her old friend Gordon Clark used to carry.

West confirmed that a moment later when he said, "I admit, it would be ironic to kill Faith Bold with her friend's gun and kill her dog with her own gun. Maybe I'll do that when the time comes. Fortunately for you, or perhaps unfortunately, the time hasn't come. Feel free to sit." He nodded with his head to the rolling office chair in front of Faith's desk. "I'd like you to be comfortable while we talk."

"I'll stand, thanks."

"No, you won't. I'd like for Turk to remain alive, but if I have to kill him to get you to comply, I will."

"If you kill him, I guarantee I won't comply."

"Then you'll die in a manner very unworthy of you."

Faith looked into his calm, hateful eyes and slowly headed for the chair.

West looked much the same as he always did. His beard was longer, and he didn't have glasses on, but he had the same deceptively benign smile and the ever-present woolen vest over a long-sleeved shirt, though the vest, like his beard, showed signs of neglect.

"You look terrible," she exaggerated. "Homelessness has done a number on you."

He shrugged. "The price I have to pay. It's not the first time I've been homeless. Sit."

She sat on the edge of her chair, resting on the balls of her feet, and prepared to leap at a moment's notice. West regarded her and sighed. "I wondered for a moment if I would ever see you again. I have to admit, I've greatly underestimated your Agency's capacity for hunting people. Even with the Marshals withdrawing their support last month, you've managed to keep me in hiding for an embarrassingly long amount of time. If Desrouleaux had gotten his way, your home would still be under surveillance."

Faith's lips thinned at that. She had been the one to tell Desrouleaux to send the agents away. She'd thought about asking for protection again after the spike in attacks from street thugs, but she hadn't ended up following through.

And she'd forgotten to set the barricade. She'd been so distracted by her thoughts that she hadn't rearmed the barricade or set her alarm. Of Course, that would be the one time she actually needed it.

No, she didn't believe in coincidence. West must have been watching and waiting for her to make exactly the mistake she had just made.

And once more, she was at his mercy.

"Why did you send people after me?" she asked. "Why hire street thugs?"

He grinned evilly. "To let you know that I care. I knew it would be some time before I could visit personally, so I sent you some friends as a token of my appreciation. I'm sorry to hear that you didn't love them as much as I did. Two of them were quite upset with me after the beating you gave them. They said I neglected to mention how dangerous the target was. Not in so many words, of course. I didn't really hire professionals."

"That's what I mean," Faith said. If she could keep him talking, she could buy herself time to figure out a plan. "Why send such unprofessional people after me. Did you not think I could protect myself from them?"

"I wasn't trying to kill you. I only wanted you to know that I was thinking of you."

"How sweet," she replied drily.

He laughed and said, "Well, I do what I can to show my affection."

"So why are you here now?"

"Because. I think it's time we drew our little game to conclusion. I'll admit this isn't how I hoped things would end. I had a plan to wear you down little by little until you broke mentally. I wasn't even going to kill you. I was going to make you watch helplessly while I took everyone else from you. I was going to kill the vet, then I was going to kill your dog, and then last, I was going to take your Prince. I was going to disappear after that and leave you searching fruitlessly for the rest of your life.

"But fate decided to intervene. The vet survived the beating I gave him. My mistake, of course. I should have shot him. Turk woke before I could stab him. Another mistake. I *really* should have learned to appreciate guns more. The FBI started becoming halfway competent, and I was unable to leave hiding for a long time. I doubt I'll be able to survive in the open for much longer."

West was eleven feet away. Faith could reach behind, grab her computer monitor and throw it at his head in less than a second. *Thank God for wireless.* Then she would hit the ground and hope that West aimed high. She could close the distance to him in about two seconds, hopefully not long enough for him to recover from the pain of having a twelve-pound brick of glass and hard plastic hitting his face. If Turk moved at exactly the same time, he could evade the gunshot as well.

God, it was so close. There was no margin for error.

There was also no choice.

"So," West continued, "I'm afraid I'll have to satisfy myself with just killing both of you and take as my payment the looks of frustration I see on both of you now. It's a bitter pill to swallow. I wanted so much to do what Trammell couldn't do and break you. Instead, I must be content to do something else he couldn't do and kill you."

"Now, Turk!"

Faith spun and threw the monitor, dropping to the floor as she did. The corner of the monitor struck West just below his eye. He cried out and fired both weapons. One thudded into the wall just above Faith's leg. The other punched through the door to the closet, slicing the air where Turk had stood a moment ago.

Turk leaped for West, but the killer threw himself sideways over the bed. He snarled and fired twice, but Faith and Turk both changed directions just in time, Turk pushing forward off of the wall rather than backward and Faith pivoting and launching at West.

She grabbed his right wrist, and Turk latched onto his left. He snarled again and threw her, dragging him effortlessly. God, how was he so strong? His arm felt like a steel cable!

He swung and flailed, but Faith held on grimly to his wrist and Turk dug into this opposite hand, enduring the blows as West slammed him against the wall and tried to shake him onto the floor.

West lifted his right leg to kick at Faith, and Faith instantly took advantage, dropping her weight and kicking out his other foot. He fell on top of her, and for a terrifying instant, the barrel of Clark's gun was pointing straight at her.

She jerked her head to the side just as West fired. She felt a pop as her right eardrum ruptured and gasped with the pain that shredded through her head.

West bared his teeth and shifted his weight, putting his knee on her belly. Turk planted all four of his feet and pulled hard, yanking West off of Faith and sending him falling onto his back.

The movement tore his arm away from Faith, however. Instead of aiming at Faith again, West aimed at Turk.

"No!"

Faith slammed her shoulder into his wrist, and West's third shot opened a hole in the ceiling. She put her knee on his chest and grabbed his elbow with one hand and the slide of the gun with the other. He struggled underneath her, but Turk put his weight down on West's stomach and began twisting his head from left to right, savaging West's arm.

West screamed in pain but maintained a death grip on both weapons. They needed to hurt him somehow. As long as he was conscious, he wasn't letting go.

She got to her feet and with Turk's help dragged West away from the wall. He yanked his left hand around and fired, the round missing Faith's leg by an inch.

With a yell, she lifted her right leg high and brought her knee down hard on West's nose. She heard a satisfying crack as the bone shattered.

West cried out again, but he still wouldn't let go of the damned handguns. Faith lifted her leg again and drove it down onto the pulped mess of his nose. Once more, he screamed, but wouldn't let go. She heard sirens outside and screeching tires. Someone had called the police.

She lifted her leg a third time, and he met her eyes. The hate in his gaze was so strong, it was almost tangible.

With a strangled roar, he yanked his left arm up and threw Turk off of him. Turk's teeth tore his flesh, leaving his arm in tatters, but leaving the gun free.

Faith brought her right arm over to grab his left wrist and shifted her left hand up to grab his right. She planted her right knee hard in his sternum, but he still overpowered her, rolling her onto her back. She kicked with her right leg, but he shifted his hips and landed in between her legs. She tried to roll out from under him, but he growled and lifted his left hand high, weakening her grip on it.

Turk launched at him again, grabbing his wrist and yanking backward, trying to break his arm. West pulled forward and rolled Turk onto his back underneath him. At the same time, he tore his right arm from Faith's grasp.

With a snarl of triumph, he pointed both weapons down at the two of them.

"Drop the weapons!"

Faith looked to her bedroom door to see two police officers holding their weapons on West. They looked young, maybe in their mid to late twenties. They also looked terrified.

But they held their weapons steadily and aimed directly at West.

"Drop it now!"

Faith turned back to West, expecting to see rage in his face. She also expected him to kill her and Turk as a last act before dying himself.

Instead, she saw him smiling with something that looked like victory. Blood poured from his ruined arm and his shattered nose, but he grinned at Faith.

"Remember. I *will* break you."

He dropped the weapons and sat up, lifting his hands high. Turk immediately rolled over and grabbed his shoulder, dragging West to the ground off of Faith. He held him there until the police officers came inside and took over.

When West was handcuffed, one of the officers led him outside while the other knelt by Faith. "Are you okay?" he asked. "Are you hurt?"

She shook her head. "I'm fine. I'm a little roughed up, but not too bad."

"We'll get medical here to have a look at you and your dog," he said. He looked back toward the living room. "Hey, was that—"

"Yes," Faith said. "You two just collared Franklin West."

The officer's eyes grew big as saucers. "Holy shit," he breathed. "Holy shit."

He stood and helped Faith to his feet. Then he shivered. He smiled sheepishly at her. "Sorry. I just… wow."

"Yeah," Faith agreed. "I hear you."

She followed the officer outside. West was sitting in the back of their police cruiser. He looked at Faith and smiled again.

Faith should have felt relieved. West was in custody, and as dangerous as he was, the chances of him escaping the type of custody they would place him in were nonexistent.

But the gleam in his eyes robbed her of that relief and instead sent a chill of fear through her.

Remember. I will *break you.*

EPILOGUE

"He was *here?*"

Michael stared at Faith, wide-eyed with shock. Faith was getting tired of seeing that expression.

"Yes, he was. You missed him by fourteen minutes."

"Damn." Michael stood and looked down the street. "I think I passed the cruiser they took him in."

"You probably did."

Faith sat on the steps in front of her apartment. Turk was glued to her side, his eyes shifting everywhere, prepared to eliminate any threat that presented itself.

EMS had just released Faith. She had minor bruising, but that was it. Turk had a more serious bruise to his left hip, but Faith had declined a hospital trip for both of them. Turk had survived far worse than a bruise, and in any case, the only way to get him to leave her side right now was to sedate him.

She had called Michael immediately after speaking to the officers and confirming West's identity. He, of course, had come right over.

"Did you call the Boss yet?"

"PD did. He's flagged in their system since he's number one on the Most Wanted list. He'll be in Bureau custody within an hour."

"Damn." Michael shook his head. Then he grinned at Faith. "Look at you. You finally did it. You caught Franklin West."

"Actually, Officers Mulvaney and Galveston did. He was about to… well, he had guns to our heads when they showed up."

"Hey." Michael put a hand on her shoulder and looked her directly in the eye. "You won, okay? He's in our hands now. He's never going to hurt you again."

Faith smiled and thanked him, but she didn't correct herself because she was afraid to say that West was about to kill them. She corrected herself because she wasn't sure if he wanted to kill them or if this was somehow all part of her plan."

"The neighbors called it in?" Michael asked after a moment.

"I assume so. He fired four rounds in the unit."

And missed every time. Barely, but still, they had gotten very lucky right up until the moment before the cops had arrived.

Well, it didn't matter, did it? He was in custody now. What plan could he possibly have that would help him when he was shackled, hogtied and placed in the shoe until his trial ended and he was sent to an even sturdier SHU in Florence?

Faith tried to tell herself it was over, but something wouldn't let her believe it.

Michael's phone rang. He checked it and said, "The Boss. Probably to talk to you." He answered and said, "Prince. Yep. She's right here, Turk too. They look fine. A few bruises, but West's nose looks like stir fry and his left arm looks like chow mein, so they got the better end of the deal. I'm guessing Desrouleaux and Chavez are heading over to the precinct to do the pickup?" He paused a second, then said. "Sure. I'll bring her over." He looked at Faith. "You mind coming to the office for a debrief? I think he just doesn't trust that I'm telling him the truth when I said you're all right."

Faith chuckled softly. "Sure, I'll head over."

"Cool." He put the phone to his ear and said, "Yeah, we're on our way. Do me a favor, get the guys to brew some good coffee, and if there's any food that doesn't look like it came out of a donkey's ass, can they warm it up for her? Or wait, does Shanahan's deliver this time of night, er… morning? Okay, we'll do that, then. You can put it on my card, I'll text you the number. Cool. Thanks, Boss, see you soon."

He looked at Faith. "You've got good coffee and an even better sandwich waiting for you. I'll order Turk a Super Beef Hoagie too. Don't roll your eyes at me, this is how I show my love for you."

Faith laughed and said, "Sounds good. Thank you."

"No worries. Hey, smile! We did it! The bastard's off the streets!" Faith smiled, and he said, "Much better."

***

Faith didn't think she would be able to eat, but when she saw the sandwich on the Boss's desk, she tore into it with an almost feral hunger. The Boss waited patiently for her to slow down. His face wore a strange look, and it took Faith a moment to figure out that it was compassion.

"How are you feeling?" he asked her.

"Have you ever asked me that before?" she replied.

“I have, believe it or not. Once every five or six years, I stop being an asshole for ten minutes.”

She chuckled and said, “I don’t think you’re an asshole.

“You do, but that’s okay. You respect me, and that’s more important.”

She rolled her eyes. “That sounds more like the Boss I know.”

“You haven’t answered my question.”

She sighed. “I’m… well, it’s surreal. I don’t know how to react.”

He nodded. “Yeah, I understand that.” He sighed and took his seat. “Okay, so the official reason I have you here. With West in custody and your intimate association with him… God, that sounds horrible. Let me rephrase. With your experience with him, you’re going to be a big part of the Bureau’s case. I know you know this, so I won’t bore you with details right now. I’ll just tell you that you should expect to be harassed at all hours by Legal for a while. I’ll do my best to shoo them away, but I’m afraid you’re about to be exposed to the worst part of being a Federal Agent: dealing with lawyers and judges.”

Faith smiled drily. “I’ve dealt with them before.”

“Not like this. Not that it’s going to be as big a deal as having Trammell’s disciple running around thinking of ways to torture you. Speaking of, I just talked to Desrouleaux. West is currently shackled like Hannibal Lecter and on his way to the FBI detention center next door. We’re going to put him under the same guard we put terrorists under, so he’s not going anywhere. I know you’re going to want to talk to him, and you’ll get your chance, but not for at least three weeks. You’re going to take those three weeks and do something that has nothing to do with the FBI.”

Faith started to protest, and he lifted his hand. “This isn’t up for discussion. Good thing or not, you’re not going to be in the right frame of mind to do your job for a while. If you don’t want to believe that I actually care about your mental health, believe that I care about your performance as an agent. So go somewhere, take your boyfriend with you, and pretend to be a normal person for a little while. Take Turk too. Let him chase squirrels instead of killers.”

She grinned at him. “What do you have against squirrels all of a sudden?”

“One of them stole my bag of kettle chips out of my hand yesterday. I’m going to bring the wrath of God down on their fluffy little asses.”

Faith burst into laughter and for the first time in her memory, she heard the Boss laugh too.

When his laughter subsided, he wiped tears from his eyes and said, “Oh, God. I needed that. It’s been too long.”

He stood and held out his hand. “Well, Bold. It is my pleasure to congratulate you on the capture of Franklin West, the Copycat Donkey Killer. Even if you weren’t the one to capture him.”

She took his hand and said, "Thank you, sir," but her smile was far from genuine.

Something in West’s eyes when the police led him away told her this wasn’t over yet.

Remember. I will *break you.*

NOW AVAILABLE!

SO SILENT
(A Faith Bold Mystery—Book 15)

When an eerie high-frequency pitch is the calling card of a methodical killer, FBI Agent Faith Bold and her canine companion are thrust into a deadly game of silence and screams. Can Faith and Turk break the code before the next victim hears their final note?

"A masterpiece of thriller and mystery."
—Books and Movie Reviews, Roberto Mattos (re Once Gone)

SO SILENT is Book #15 in a long-anticipated new series by #1 bestseller and USA Today bestselling author Blake Pierce, whose bestseller Once Gone (a free download) has received over 7,000 five star ratings and reviews.

FBI Special Agent Faith Bold doesn't believe she can ever return to the force after the trauma she's been through. Suffering from past demons, she feels unfit for duty and content to retire—until Turk walks into her life.

Turk, a former Marine Corps dog, wounded in battle, suffers from his own demons. But he never lets it show as he gives everything to Faith to get her back on her feet.

Each are slow to warm up to each other, but when they do, they are inseparable. Each is equally determined to hunt down the demons chasing them, whatever the cost, and to watch each other's backs—even at the risk of their own life.

A page-turning and harrowing crime thriller featuring a brilliant and tortured FBI agent, the Faith Bold series is a riveting mystery, packed with non-stop action, suspense, twists and turns, revelations, and driven by a breakneck pace that will keep you flipping pages late into the night. Fans of Rachel Caine, Teresa Driscoll and Robert Dugoni are sure to fall in love.